First American Edition 2020
Kane Miller, A Division of EDC Publishing

Text © Alesha Dixon, 2018
Cover design by Kat Godard, Dradog
Cover characters and inside illustrations by James Lancett
represented by the Bright Agency © Scholastic, 2018
The right of Alesha Dixon to be identified as
the author of this Work has been asserted by her.

First published in the UK by Scholastic Ltd., 2018
This edition published under license from Scholastic Ltd.

For information contact:
Kane Miller, A Division of EDC Publishing
PO Box 470663
Tulsa, OK 74147-0663
www.kanemiller.com
www.usbornebooksandmore.com
www.edcpub.com

Library of Congress Control Number: 2019946984
Printed and bound in the United States of America
1 2 3 4 5 6 7 8 9 10
ISBN: 978-1-68464-079-9

LIGHTNING Girl

SUPERHERO SQUAD

ALESHA DIXON

In collaboration with Katy Birchall
Illustrated by James Lancett

Kane Miller
A DIVISION OF EDC PUBLISHING

For my real life superhero!
My light and my love, Azuka.

THE WEEKL

LIGHT
LIGHTN

Aurora Beam

She may be Beam by surname, but
superhero Aurora seemed to have
nothing to smile about on Tuesday
morning!

Leaving her house accompanied
her father, Professor Henry Be
Aurora – known globally as Ligh
Girl due to her incredible ab

HERALD

EN UP,
NG GIRL!

...rs a frown about town!

...al Report by Olive Folio

...ot dazzling light beams from her
...alms – appeared shy and overwhelmed
...by the press assembled outside her
house.

    Although the *Weekly Herald* cannot
confirm the cause of her frown, there
has been speculation that she was on her
way to the dentist.

"Perhaps she was nervous about
needing a filling, if that's where she was
going," one witness said after the
incident. "But superheroes like Lightning Girl need to lead by example and
frowning isn't something to look up to."

    The *Weekly Herald* has contacted Aurora
Beam's spokesperson for comment.

THE DAILY

SUPERH

Lightning Girl suff
after

Aurora Beam, a.k.a. Lightning Girl, walked straight into a door this morning after mistaking a "pull" sign for a "push" one, the *Daily Scope* c exclusively reveal.

The famous superhero, re for capturing the notorious

SCOPE

RO FAIL!

s MAJOR embarrassment
lking into door!

e Report by Henry Nib

glar earlier this year and soon to be

unching her own range of nutritious

cereal bars, had been opening the door

of a café with her German shepherd

dog, Kimmy, when the unfortunate

incident occurred.

"There was a loud thud as she

walked into the door," a witness

revealed. "I was sitting in the café at

the time and you just saw her face hit

the glass square on. I had no idea

superheroes could be so clumsy."

The *Daily Scope* has contacted Aurora

Beam's representative for comment.

ut

Suddenly, my foot slipped.

There was a loud gasp as I managed to just find my grip in time, stopping me from falling through the air. I clung on for dear life, my arm beginning to ache and my legs dangling. Finally, I found a foothold and hauled myself up into a stable position. I looked down at my audience and gulped.

"Don't look down, Aurora!" Kizzy cried, standing on the ground directly beneath me, my dog, Kimmy, at her side. They both seemed miles away. "Remember, you're a superhero! You can do this!"

I nodded and lifted my gaze to meet that of my enemy. He was just a few feet away. He spotted me and immediately narrowed his eyes to threatening slits.

"I can do this," I whispered, repeating my best friend's encouraging words. "I CAN DO THIS."

I reached out toward him. He recoiled from my fingertips before swiping his arm at me. I just managed to pull my hand away in time, letting out a yelp as I tried to regain my balance.

"I can't do this!" I wailed. "It's all over!"

There was a deathly silence as Kizzy let my words sink in.

And then she burst out laughing.

"Oh, for goodness' sake." Kizzy giggled, shaking her head. "It's only a cat. And

2

according to his owner, Mister Salmon is usually very friendly. Just grab him and get him down here. You've been up in that tree for twenty minutes."

Mister Salmon looked quite content sitting on the branch next to mine, licking his paw, blissfully unaware of the chaos he was causing. I repositioned my feet on the branch and stretched my arm forward again, determined to complete the mission of rescuing this cat from this tree.

He took another swipe at me with his razor-sharp claws, hissing loudly. I let out a long sigh.

Being a superhero was REALLY overrated.

Ever since the world found out about my superpowers a few months ago, I had been in such high demand that I hadn't had time to think.

When I first discovered my weird ability to shoot powerful light beams out of my hands halfway through the spring term, I had been sworn to secrecy by Mum. It turned out that she didn't have a boring office job, like she'd always told me. She was, in fact, a superhero, saving the world on a daily basis.

So all those times she'd come home with her hair on fire and scorch marks on her face, she hadn't just returned from "an invigorating class of hot yoga" like she'd claimed. She had actually been busy stopping someone evil from taking over the world.

Yeah. It had been a lot to take in.

Mum had gone on to explain how every woman in my family has superpowers, including her twin sister, Lucinda, and their mum, Nanny Beam. As if that wasn't completely overwhelming, I also had to get my head round the legend about how the Beam superpowers came about in the first place: when the planet was plunged into a strange darkness, centuries ago, my ancestor Dawn Beam harnessed the powers of the most precious stone you can imagine, the Light of the World, and lit up the Earth once more.

Then those magical powers were passed to her daughter and then *her* daughter, and so on and so forth, through every female Beam until you get to … well, me.

It has always been the responsibility of the Beam women to use their powers of summoning light to secretly protect and save the world from darkness.

But I kind of messed up the whole secrecy thing due to a *minor* incident when lots of people witnessed my superpowers. I stopped my evil science teacher, Mr. Mercury, who was really the notorious Blackout Burglar, from stealing all the precious stones, including the Light of the World, from an exhibition at the Natural History Museum.

I should have guessed that Mr. Mercury was a bad guy right from when he first arrived at our school in January. There were so many signs that we missed. For a start, he gave me detention ALL THE TIME for no reason whatsoever.

(OK, yes, I did *accidentally* kick a ball at his head and, fine, once I knocked his food all down his shirt. Oh, wait, and that time I flicked blue ink at him. Then I almost destroyed a room on a school trip. And I never listened to a word he said because his voice was so dull.

But aside from that, no reason whatsoever.)

Now we know why he chose being a science teacher as his disguise – he got a job at our school so that he could ask my dad, who was the professor in charge of the precious stones exhibition, to give us a school tour of the Natural History Museum; the perfect opportunity for him to scout out how best to steal the stones without anyone suspecting him.

Thanks to Kizzy, who worked out his evil plan in the nick of time, we were able to stop him from getting away with the precious stones, although we still don't know who he was working for. Not even my dad had known just how precious one of the stones in the collection was, but someone out there knew *exactly* what it was. They had paid Mr. Mercury to steal the gems, promising him that he could have them all except for one – the Light of the World.

We'd only worked it out after Mr. Mercury had been arrested and Mum and Dad realized the symbol on the stone matched the glowing scar on my palm. Mr. Mercury is now safely behind bars in a London prison but, to this day, he has refused to give up the name of the person he was working for and we have no idea how they know about the Light of the World, or why its pattern matches my scar.

It is all a bit creepy, to be honest.

Anyway, after that evening my picture was suddenly all over the Internet with bold headlines declaring:

| HOME | NEWS | SPORTS | WEATHER |

LIGHTNING GIRL SAVES THE DAY!

Report by Jennifer Scoop

My secret wasn't so secret anymore. Everything changed.

I instantly became one of the most popular girls in my class. I was asked for selfies with both students AND teachers during lessons throughout the entire summer term, never getting a moment to myself. I felt like I was being watched, in the hope that I might do something super extraordinary at any moment.

Which, by the way, made things like tripping over my own feet even more embarrassing.

"You're a celebrity now," Kizzy said with a laugh, when the headmistress asked if I approved of the name the school committee had chosen for the newly refurbished science wing: the Lightning Girl Laboratories.

I was so relieved when summer vacation started, but it just got worse.

Now that I wasn't in school and had some free time, I was constantly getting calls from people all over the country, desperately needing my help with cases, like this one with Mister Salmon. Cats stuck up in trees ... again and again; walkers who had accidentally gotten their foot caught down a rabbit hole; tricky light bulbs that needed changing; pigeons trapped in the London Underground, flying around in a panic; and drivers in traffic jams, looking for advice on a better route.

The closest I've ever been to a vaguely exciting incident was when I was called to a haunted hotel last week, but it turned out to just be an owl stuck in the air vents, hooting mournfully.

At least that mission didn't involve heights.

"Mister Salmon is being very stubborn," I informed Kizzy, looking longingly at the ladder. "Maybe we should just leave him here and he'll come down on his own."

Kizzy didn't look up from her phone.

"No, according to his owner and the neighbors, he's been up there a good few hours meowing in distress."

I raised an eyebrow while Mister Salmon calmly cleaned his whiskers. "He doesn't look in distress to me!"

"Well, we have to get him down in the next ten minutes otherwise we're going to be behind schedule." Kizzy held her phone up so that I could see the spreadsheet on her screen before tapping her watch impatiently. "You're needed on the other side of town soon. You're opening a new bus stop. So grab Mister Salmon and shimmy back on down the ladder."

"Huh?" I leaned against the tree trunk, pulling a leaf from my hair.

"What does opening a bus stop even mean?"

"It means that they've built a brand-new bus stop and they want you to cut the ribbon to declare it officially open for use. A lot of papers are sending journalists."

I grimaced at the idea of photographers and reporters. I still wasn't used to all the media attention. It was so weird to see photos of me online with captions like the one I saw yesterday: *"Superhero Aurora Beam takes her energetic German shepherd, Kimmy, for a walk, without realizing that she has toilet paper stuck to her shoe! Read below for more on this exclusive story!"*

My brother, Alexis, read that and then laughed solidly for about ten minutes before printing out loads of copies of the photo and sticking them EVERYWHERE around the house.

And I mean *everywhere*. I even found a copy taped to the inside of the dishwasher.

"Let me get this straight," I said to Kizzy. "Reporters want a photo of me cutting a ribbon to open a bus stop?"

"Yep."

"I didn't realize opening bus stops was a thing."

"It certainly is."

"According to who?"

"According to your personal assistant."

"Ah." I sighed, admitting defeat. "Well, in that case, I'll be there. My PA is always right."

"And don't you forget it."

I caught Kizzy's eye and we both broke into wide grins. I never actually asked Kizzy to be my PA; she just decided one day that she was and that was that. She was brilliant at it, too, because she was so organized.

"Come on, Mister Salmon," I pleaded, turning my attention back to the cat. "Did you hear Kizzy? If you don't let me rescue you, then a new bus stop won't be opened on time. It would be a DISASTER!"

"I can hear your sarcasm from down here, you know," Kizzy told me, sharing a look with Kimmy before giving her a pat on the head. "Maybe Kimmy is putting off Mister Salmon. Should I take her around the corner out of sight or something?"

"And leave me stuck here in a tree on my own?"

"Mister Salmon is the one who is stuck. You're meant to be the rescuer." Kizzy crouched down to tickle Kimmy's chin. "Maybe Mister Salmon is scared of dogs."

Kimmy rolled onto her back, letting her tongue loll out, so that Kizzy could scratch her belly.

"Yeah, she looks really ferocious," I said, rolling my eyes. "Right, Mister Salmon, if I edge a bit closer..."

I shuffled along the branch, ignoring the worrying creaking sound coming from under my feet, and then reached out to grasp the branch that Mister Salmon was contentedly perched on, careful not to shake it and frighten him. Edging nearer, I calmly stretched my other arm out and in one quick movement, swept my hand under his tummy and pulled him safely into my chest.

He yowled loudly and immediately began to scramble and scratch to get free from my grip.

"Stop ... doing ... that..." I gasped, clinging to him with one arm while using the other to balance myself as I made my way back along the branch toward the ladder. "I'm ... trying ... to ... save ... you!"

As I got onto the first rung he clawed free, scaling my legs to hop down the ladder before landing neatly on the ground. He eyed Kimmy suspiciously, looked back up at me still in the tree and gave one last hiss before pouncing away across the grass toward his home down the street.

His owner, who had been watching from a safe distance on his front lawn, opened his arms and swept Mister Salmon into a giant hug.

"Thank you!" he yelled, as the grumpy Mister Salmon attempted to wriggle away from his enthusiastic nuzzling. "Thank you so much!"

"Well done, Aurora!" Kizzy smiled, watching them while I made my way back down the ladder. "You see? You really are a truly brilliant superhero."

Just as she came to the end of her sentence, my foot slipped forward and I lost my grip on the rung I was holding on to.

Oh. Noooooooooo.

I yelped as both my legs went flying forward

through the gap, while the rest of me went toppling backward, so that I ended up dangling upside down, my legs hooked around the rung I was supposed to have stepped elegantly onto.

I desperately grappled at the sides of the ladder to try and pull myself back up, but they were too slippery.

There was a brief pause before Kizzy exploded into uncontrollable laughter.

"Help! It's not funny!" I exclaimed. "Kizzy!"

"I'm sorry," she wheezed, clutching her stomach. "But you should have seen your face! That seemed to happen in slow motion! Are you OK?"

"No. I am not OK!" I huffed, although her laughter was so infectious that I couldn't stop myself from smiling. "Can you please come and help me down?"

She walked toward the ladder and stood in front of me, bursting into a fresh round of giggles as she realized my face was level with her knees.

I folded my arms, which is, I found out, quite difficult to do when you're dangling upside down. "Are you finished?"

She opened her mouth to answer but was interrupted by excited screams coming from a group of girls running down the road toward us.

"LIGHTNING GIRL!" one of them was shouting, pointing at me and looking at the others. "I told you it was her! Quick!"

"This. Can't. Be. Happening," I said under my breath.

The girls came racing over with their phones, jostling with each other so they could crouch next to me and get selfies with me while I dangled there. "We're your biggest fans!" they kept saying, cramming in for a group photo.

"Kizzy," I hissed, as the girls argued over the best filter to use on the next photo. "The blood is kind of going to my head here."

Kizzy cleared her throat. "All right, thanks so much, everyone, but Lightning Girl has a busy schedule and she's ... uh ... in a bit of a situation right now that she needs to ... sort out, so if you could all move along..."

They groaned in disappointment as Kizzy ushered them on their way. I tried to keep smiling as though I was perfectly at ease about hanging by my knees the wrong way up, and it was all part of my plan, aware that they were glancing back every now and then from the road.

"Right, now that your fans are gone," Kizzy said, clapping her hands together, "let's get you down from there."

"Finally. And, Kizzy?"

"Yes?"

"You don't think they'll show anyone those photos, do you? Of me stuck upside down on a ladder, I mean."

"No, course not," Kizzy smiled warmly, as her phone began to beep incessantly in her pocket. "No one will ever know."

★

BREAKING NEWS BULLETIN: LIGHTNING GIRL STUCK ON LADDER!

Click on the link below to go to our website and view a full video and more photos of this HILARIOUS superhero mishap!

Z

"Aurora? Aurora, wake up!"

Someone shook me awake. I blinked the sleep out of my eyes. I could just make out a load of blurred faces looming toward me.

"AHHHHHHHHHHHH!"

I screamed in fright and instinctively my powers rushed through me, bursting from my hands and brightening the room.

"Aurora!" someone yelled. "It's us!"

"Kizzy?"

I quickly brought my powers under control. "What's going on?"

I realized I was at the kitchen table and Mum and Dad were there, along with my best friends from school: Kizzy, Suzie, Georgie and Fred. They had all flung themselves to the floor at my sudden light-beam outburst and were slowly getting to their feet. Kimmy was so distressed by what had just happened that she ran outside to bark at the sky.

"I told you, I should just have woken her gently on my own," Mum said pointedly to Dad. "I knew she'd get a fright."

I rubbed my aching neck. "What happened?"

"You must have fallen asleep at the table," Dad said gently. "Again."

"I hate it when you don't give any warning before blasting out your powers like that," Suzie groaned at me, lifting her hands to her hair to check that her sleek blond ponytail was still as neat as usual.

"I could have broken my ankle when I ducked those light beams, and then my blossoming gymnastics career would be completely over!"

"It's not exactly Aurora's fault," Georgie reasoned, winking at me. "She did get woken up by a big crowd all standing round her. That's got to be pretty scary."

"Not as scary as the time someone dared me to eat the hottest chili pepper in the world," Fred said, giving Kimmy a scratch behind her ears when she came back into the kitchen. "It nearly blew my head off."

"Oh please." Suzie sighed, rolling her eyes and straightening her sweater. "You can't even handle a mild curry."

"Yes, I can," Fred huffed.

"No, you ca—"

"Anyway," Kizzy interrupted, smiling at me, "we should probably tell Aurora why we're all here."

"What time is it?" I asked, blinking at the sunlight shining in through the windows. "I don't remember falling asleep. I'm so confused."

"It's three in the afternoon. You did your magazine photo shoot this morning, remember?" Kizzy prompted. "Then you had lunch with the mayor, and *then* you said you needed to pop home to grab your new Lightning Girl jacket—"

"Speaking of which, does it fit OK?" Georgie asked.

"Perfectly," I said. "Thanks for designing it for me. It looks so cool with the sneakers."

"You're very talented when it comes to accessorizing," Mum added.

"I feel lucky being able to design Lightning Girl's personal accessories," Georgie replied, blushing.

It was weird to think how nervous I used

to feel around Georgie Taylor and Suzie Bravo. Georgie has always been the coolest girl in school. Her mum was a publicist for some of the biggest fashion brands, so Georgie always had the latest bags and more – but then she'd add her own touch, making them totally unique and even cooler.

Her best friend Suzie, the gymnastics whiz, was equally as popular. She loved to entertain everyone with her amazing gymnastic skills, cartwheeling through the classroom to rapturous adoring applause. The only person in our class who wasn't afraid of Suzie, aside from Georgie, was Fred, the class joker. Suzie was his favorite person in the world to play pranks on – and that hadn't changed, even now that they were friends.

Georgie, Suzie, Fred and Kizzy found out about my superpowers before anyone else, completely by accident. I thought they were going to call me a big freak and get me expelled, but instead they thought it was kind of cool and formed a secret superhero club, called the Bright Sparks, so that I would never have to face any danger alone.

Although, since the precious stones rescue at the Natural History Museum, the Bright Sparks hadn't had all that much to do. Our superhero meetings mainly involved eating pizza and watching movies. But still.

"Why was I getting my lightning-bolt jacket, Kizzy?" I yawned.

"To wear it during the photo shoot for your new cereal bar, Lightning Crunch, which started an hour ago. I've been calling and calling."

"Oh no," I groaned, burying my head in my hands as things became a bit less hazy. "I'm sorry. I remember now. I sat down at the kitchen table to tie my shoelaces" – I glanced at my undone shoes – "and I must have just fallen asleep mid-tying."

"I'm not surprised," Dad said, sitting down at the table opposite me. "You haven't stopped the past few weeks. All these events and rescue missions."

Mum nodded in agreement, resting a hand on his shoulder. It may have only seemed like a small gesture, but seeing my parents acting like a team made me feel so happy. They had separated around the time I discovered my powers. It had been horrible.

But I guess it had been horrible for Mum and Dad too because they realized that they couldn't be without each other. Mum had gradually moved her things back into the house and now they seemed to be stronger than ever.

I asked Mum recently how things were with Dad and she got this gooey look in her eyes and went, "Oh, he's so handsome, isn't he?"

It was gross. In a good way.

"Have you been on Snapchat?" Suzie asked, interrupting my thoughts. "They've created a new Lightning Girl filter. It is so cool. It shoots lightning bolts out of your head."

"But my lightning bolts come out of my hands."

"Whatever." She sighed dreamily. "A Snapchat filter means you've truly made it."

"And a cereal bar named after you DEFINITELY means you've made it," Fred added.

Kizzy smiled, getting out her phone. "Which brings us nicely to why we're all here. An opportunity has come up—"

"Whoa, what am I missing?" The kitchen door opened and my brother came in, acknowledging everyone with a wave before heading straight for the fridge. "This looks like an important meeting."

"Alexis," Mum said, exasperated. "Why are you still in your pajamas? It is the middle of the afternoon."

"So? It's summer vacation." He took several glugs of coconut water straight from the bottle.

"Ew! Alexis!" I huffed. "You're putting your germs all over it!"

"Better than almost taking out the house with uncontrollable light beams. I felt the energy blast all the way up in my room and saw the flash of light under my door – it distracted me from my project. I thought you were supposed to be able to handle your powers by now," he replied. "Maybe you need to take Aurora's superhero training up a notch, Mum."

"I'll have you know she is completely in control of her superpowers," Mum said defensively. "But we haven't had much time to squeeze in training recently, what with all her media appearances and things, and she's overtired and—"

"What's happening?" My little sister, Clara, appeared at Alexis's side holding a science textbook. "No offense, but you're all being very loud and I'm trying to study DNA."

"It's summer vacation. And aren't you only seven years old?" Suzie asked, baffled.

"Yeah. Why?"

"Hang on," Dad interjected, narrowing his eyes at Alexis. "What project?"

"Huh?"

"You just said that Aurora's light beams distracted you from your project. What project?"

Alexis shuffled his feet. "Nothing. It's nothing. Just a thing. A nothing thing. Nothing."

"Alexis," Dad growled, "what are you up to now?"

"Yeah, Alexis, what are you up to now?"

Fred grinned in excitement.

Everyone at school knew that Alexis had a knack for both technology and big trouble. He was always in detention for something, like hacking into the school computer system and changing his grades, or the time he sent around a mass email to parents and students, declaring that the school was closed for the week while they dealt with a "rodent infestation."

The teachers spent the whole of Monday morning wondering where everyone was until they worked out what had happened. We all got the day off and Alexis was suspended for two days – which, in his eyes, was a win because *technically* he got three days off.

"Change of subject, anyone?" Alexis asked the room as Dad glared at him.

"How about we finally tell Aurora what we're all doing here," Georgie suggested, while

Alexis dodged Dad's eye contact.

"Aurora, you've been invited on *Good Morning Britain!*" Suzie exclaimed. "It is SO cool."

I blinked at her. "What?"

"I got the call about half an hour ago," Kizzy said. "They want you on the breakfast show tomorrow morning."

"Hang on, wait a minute," I said, trying to unscramble my very tired brain. "What are you talking about?"

"You know the TV show, *Good Morning Britain*? They've invited you on as a star guest," Kizzy explained. "They'll send a car to pick you up in the early hours and then you'll do a full interview. It's completely up to you whether you want to do it or not."

"Kizzy told us, and we decided that if you did go on the show, you were going to need ALL the help you could get, which is why we're here," Suzie said.

Kizzy shot her a pointed look.

"What?" Suzie shrugged. "This is national television we're talking about. Didn't you see the ladder footage? She clearly needs our help."

"What Suzie means is, we're the Bright Sparks." Georgie smiled. "We're in it together."

"What do you think, Aurora?" Mum asked.

"Uh…"

"You've been doing a lot recently and I actually think maybe you need a break from all this … fame. You look exhausted and it would be a four a.m. start."

"Four a.m.?" Alexis snorted. "Nothing could get me out of bed at four a.m."

"Hello!" Suzie cried, throwing up her hands. "It's *Good Morning Britain*! Do you know how cool it is to be invited on that show? This is a once-in-a-lifetime opportunity! I'm hoping to have a gymnastics slot right after Aurora's interview."

"I don't want to disappoint you, Suzie, but I really don't think they're going to let you do gymnastics on the show just because you happen to be in the studio," Kizzy pointed out. "They have a schedule."

"You don't know that," Suzie replied confidently. "They haven't seen my backflip yet or heard me talk about my new routine."

"They must be the only ones left on the planet," Fred added under his breath, receiving a sharp glare.

"Aurora, what do you think?" Dad asked, placing a hand gently on mine. "We'll do whatever you want."

"I don't know," I admitted.

They all waited patiently as I bit my lip, deep in thought.

"All right," I said eventually. "I'll do the interview."

"YES!" Suzie said, high-fiving Georgie.

"I'll let them know." Kizzy jumped to her feet and tapped a number into her phone.

Mum and Dad shared a look.

"What?" I asked, standing up and stretching.

"I just don't want you overdoing it, that's all," Mum said, concerned. "And being in the public eye is tiring. You need a rest."

I yawned, plodding over to the kitchen sink to splash cold water on my face in the hope it might make me feel more alive. "Mum, it's just an interview. What's the worst that could happen?"

When the shiny black car pulled into our driveway, Suzie let out a loud scream at the top of her lungs.

"Suzie!" Kizzy hissed, picking up her bag from the floor of the hallway. "You're going to wake up the whole neighborhood!"

Suzie checked her leotard and perfect ponytail one last time in the mirror, before pulling on her coat and taking a deep breath. "It's showtime."

"It's showtime for *Aurora*," Fred reminded

her, yawning and wiping sleep from his eyes. "Not for you."

I smiled nervously. "For all of us. Thanks for staying the night so you could come to this interview with me."

"Are you kidding?" Georgie laughed, as Suzie did some stretching, reaching down to touch her toes. "It's hardly a chore. The last time I saw Suzie this excited, it was when she won the gold at the Under-12s Gymnastic Nationals."

"It was actually the Under-13s and I won it three years in a row," Suzie corrected, marching toward the front door. "Are we all ready to go? Look alive, people!"

"Coming!" Mum whispered, creeping down the stairs, careful not to wake Dad or Alexis.

I knew that Clara was awake because when my alarm had gone off I'd spotted the light on under her door.

I'd opened it to find her writing some kind of formula on the whiteboard Mum and Dad got her for Christmas. "No can do," she'd shrugged when I'd told her to go back to sleep. "A problem popped into my brain and I won't be able to sleep unless I work it out."

It didn't take a genius to work out that my little sister was ... well ... a genius.

"All right, everyone," Kizzy said as Suzie opened the front door to wave at the driver and let him know we were on our way. "I'll go with Aurora, and Kiyana, you can drive the others if that's OK."

Mum gave her a salute. "Roger that."

"How come you get to go in the flashy television studio car?" Suzie grumbled.

"Because she is in charge of Aurora's schedule," Georgie pointed out. "It's lucky that they're letting all of us tag along in the first place."

Kizzy laughed. "You can come with us if

you want, Suzie. There's plenty of room, I'm sure."

Suzie squealed and clapped her hands. "Yes! Thanks, Kizzy, you're the best!"

Georgie sighed as Suzie raced toward the driver, who swung open the door for her. "She is going to be impossible today, isn't she?"

"When is she ever not impossible?" Fred yawned, following Mum to her car. "Any chance we can leave her behind?"

Kizzy and I laughed, sliding into the back seat next to Suzie, who was busy talking to the driver about how nice the leather seats were.

"How are you feeling?" Kizzy asked me, as we sped toward the London studio. It was dark still and the roads were completely empty, so it felt as though we were the only ones in the country awake.

"Fine," I gulped. "Just a bit nervous. I wish

I knew what they were going to ask me."

"You'll be great," Kizzy said encouragingly. "Just be yourself. They'll love you."

By the time we pulled up at the studio, I felt so nervous that I could barely step out of the car. It felt as though a million butterflies were fluttering about in my stomach and my limbs were so tired that every time I tried to move, it was as though I was wading through a jar of molasses.

"Wow!" Suzie exclaimed as we walked through the glass doors to the reception area. "It is just how I imagined it!"

A smartly dressed woman wearing a headset and bright-red lipstick came hurrying over to greet us, shaking my hand vigorously. "Hello! I'm Jennifer, one of the producers here. What an honor to have you on the show, Lightning Girl. Or would you rather I call you Miss Beam?"

"Aurora is great, thank you," I croaked, the

butterfly nerves now beginning to crawl up my throat.

"Let's get you to hair and makeup." She beamed, nodding at Suzie and Kizzy before Fred, Mum and Georgie came bustling through the doors. "Come on through, everyone."

Suzie immediately launched into a million questions, barely leaving Jennifer any time to answer them, as she led us past security and down to a dressing room, holding open the door for me. There was a row of chairs facing a long mirror with light bulbs all around it.

Suzie gasped. "This is just SO showbiz!"

"You're in here, Aurora," Jennifer said, ushering me through. "I'll take everyone else to the studio while you get ready. You're in great hands!"

As the door closed, a group of makeup artists and hairstylists surrounded me, leading me to a seat in front of the mirror and offering me a cup of tea before getting to work. I felt like a movie star getting ready for a premiere. They began applying powder to "remove the shine" and I found my heavy eyelids closing. It was so early, and the feeling of makeup

brushes sweeping along my cheeks was weirdly relaxing, so I just kind of let my eyes stay closed a bit longer and the next thing I knew I was jolted awake, coughing and spluttering through a cloud of hair spray.

"You drifted off there," a man chuckled, as he continued to suffocate me, spraying liberally across my curls. "Superhero work is exhausting, huh?"

There was a knock on the door and Mum poked her head round. "Can I come in?"

"Sure," he said, putting the hair spray down. "She's all ready to go."

"Hey, you look great," Mum said, perching on the dressing table as I blinked at my reflection. I was amazed to see that the dark circles under my eyes had completely vanished.

"I'm so sorry, Aurora, but I have to go," she admitted, holding up her phone. "There's been a situation with some kind of out-of-control fire-breathing robot in Essex." She let out a long sigh. "I wish bad guys would stop trying to take over the world. It's very inconvenient."

"You have to leave *now*?"

"Afraid so." Mum put her phone in her pocket. "According to my source, they've sent their very best at it so far, but to no avail. I'm needed right away."

Mum had never actually met her "source," the mysterious person who contacted her whenever she was needed to save the country. She had told me that whoever it was, they were very high up in the British Intelligence Service, but also very good at being able to keep their identity a secret from her. She'd asked to meet them face-to-face several times, but they had refused, informing her that she'd be introduced when the time was right.

Mum's still not entirely sure how they found

out about her powers in the first place all those years ago, but one day she'd received a message from an unknown number telling her about an evil scientist who had escaped from prison. All the police knew was that he was hiding in a network of pitch-black, eerie caves in Yorkshire. Mum's ability to summon light meant she'd quickly been able to find him and overpower him, and since then she had continued to get messages and phone calls with computerized voices telling her when she was needed to save the day.

She had a special message-alert tone for her source, so whenever her phone pinged in a certain way, our whole family would let out a collective groan, knowing that she'd have to rush off.

She still didn't let me join her on the dangerous types of superhero missions her source sent her on. I just had to stick with rescuing the likes of grumpy Mister Salmon.

"Listen," Mum said, leaning toward me, "I think it would be best if you didn't display your superpowers on television, OK?"

"What do you mean?"

"I mean, that if the presenters ask you to show off your light beams, tell them no."

"Why?"

Mum shrugged. "You've been under a lot of stress recently and I know you're putting up a front, but I can tell that you're not yourself. It's been a while since we did some serious training and I—"

"Mum, I am in full control of my superpowers," I said, shifting in my seat.

"I'm not saying that you're not," she replied firmly. "But, just in case, I don't think it's worth putting anyone in danger. There's no need for you to prove anything; you can just tell them what it's like to have superpowers. I don't think we should risk it. That's all I'm saying."

I sighed. "Fine."

"Great. Well, good luck, you'll be amazing. I'm sorry I won't be able to see it live, but, hey," she kissed me on the forehead, "superhero duty calls."

I was just about to wish her luck too, but by the time I opened my mouth, she'd already gone, the door swinging behind her.

Along with her light-beam power, Mum also happened to be VERY fast.

All the Beam women had extra perks alongside their powers. They weren't extra superpowers as such, just something in particular that we *excelled* at. Mum was crazily fast, while her sister had super levels of charm. I've been a victim of Aunt Lucinda's persuasive skills, accidentally aiding her in stealing a precious diamond necklace, so I can confirm that they are very effective.

Mum and I have both been trying to work out for ages what my extra skill might be. I was hoping it would be something like being able to fly, but I tried jumping from one sofa to the other last week and ended up falling flat on my face.

"You've got this warmth," Mum had said, when I asked her for the billionth time when my extra powers were going to start showing. "I don't know, Aurora, I can't explain it. There's something special about you, which I can't put my finger on yet. You just dazzle everyone."

Which sounds like one of those parenting cop-outs if you ask me.

Anyway, as cool as it is that Mum can run quick as a flash, it's kind of annoying when she leaves before you can finish your sentence.

"Aurora, there you are," Georgie said, bustling through the door. She was holding up a dress on a hanger in one hand and a pretty top in the other, with a pair of jeans slung over her elbow. "I've just come from wardrobe. These are the options I've picked out for you. What do you think?"

"Uh…" I glanced from one to the other. "I prefer the jeans."

"I agree," Georgie said in her most grown-up voice, handing them over to me. "They're very you. Throw these on and then they can get your microphone sorted."

"Aurora, are you ready to come through?" Jennifer asked, poking her head round the door as I finished getting dressed.

"She's almost there," Georgie informed her, tweaking the sleeves of the top, before standing back to get a good look.

"Cool sneakers!" Jennifer grinned, admiring

the glitter on my Lightning Girl shoes.

When Georgie was satisfied with my look, I followed Jennifer into the main studio, gawping at the cameras dotted EVERYWHERE around the room.

"Why do they need so many?" I asked Kizzy, swallowing the lump in my throat.

"To get different angles. Just ignore the cameras and focus on having a nice chat with the presenters."

Kizzy giggled and nodded toward a corner of the studio. Suzie was doing a handstand in front of the presenter Susannah Reid, who was clapping enthusiastically.

"It's so easy!" Suzie told her. "You want to try? I can teach you if you like."

There was a loud cackle from the other side of the studio, where Fred was standing with one of the props team.

"Ever since we got here, Fred and the head of props have been sharing tips with each other about how best to play pranks. Fred just showed me his backpack and it is now full of bottles of fake blood," Kizzy said, rolling her eyes. "And Georgie is busy in the costume department."

"I'm aware. The Bright Sparks seem to have taken over the show."

Kizzy grinned. "Speaking of which," she said, pulling some headphones on, "Jennifer has appointed me an honorary producer, so I'd better get into position. You head over to the sofa and they'll get your mic ready."

Feeling like a dazed child, while all my friends were completely in control, I wandered over to the cream sofa and sat down, waiting patiently as the sound woman fiddled with the wires of my microphone, attaching it carefully to my top.

I was a bit starstruck when Susannah Reid and Piers Morgan swanned over to shake my hand and sit down on the sofa with me. I had seen them so many times on television, it felt weird to have them here right in front of me in person. I suddenly felt really shy, but they were very nice and funny, telling me how excited they were to have me on the show.

I was just trying to form the words to say how pleased I was to be there, when suddenly the lights changed, the cameras swung to face us, and everyone seemed to be busy, rushing around doing last-minute checks. Someone was standing in front of me, giving me an overview about how the interview would play out, but I couldn't concentrate on what they were saying and then they didn't have time to repeat any of it.

My hands were becoming very clammy.

"Are ... are we about to go on?" I asked timidly as Piers Morgan finished some vocal exercises.

"Aaaaaaaaand," a loud voice boomed across the studio floor, "three ... two ... one ... ACTION!"

Sitting behind the cameras, Kizzy gave me a big thumbs-up as the show started and I was introduced as "the amazing Lightning Girl, the nation's favorite superhero."

The mixture of nerves and tiredness made me feel as though I was on autopilot, attempting to mirror the presenters' warm smiles. I felt a bit dizzy under the bright studio lighting as I tried my best to concentrate on their questions, wondering how they could possibly be so natural with all the red lights of the cameras blinking at them. I kept tripping over my words awkwardly and repeating myself, forgetting what I'd already said.

I didn't have to look at Kizzy's face to know that this interview was not going very well.

"So, when you're ready..." Susannah Reid smiled, looking at me expectantly.

I'd been too distracted to hear the question.

"S ... sorry?"

"In your own time," Piers nodded. "We can't wait to see these superpowers in person."

"Oh." I glanced at Kizzy in a panic. "I ... uh..."

"It's perfectly natural to be nervous." Susannah chuckled, gesturing at the row of cameras. "You can imagine what it's like trying to remember which one to look at!" She smiled at me warmly. "Whenever you're ready, Lightning Girl."

The whole studio was silent, watching me

expectantly. I felt bad going against what Mum had asked, but at the same time, I couldn't NOT do it now. It was live television. It felt like the whole world was watching me.

"OK." I nodded.

I closed my eyes and took a deep breath, lifting my palms.

It all happened very fast.

I only meant to bring out a soft light beam. I've done it a hundred times before.

But I couldn't focus properly. The studio lights were too bright, my eyelids were too heavy and my head was too muddled with nerves. I mustered all the energy I had left into shooting out the light beams, but I had no energy left to control it.

As I lifted my hands, it was as though the full force of my power came exploding out of them. The energy blast whooshed across the studio so powerfully, it was as though a lightning storm swept through the room.

The producers and cameras crashed to the ground, glass shattering everywhere, and the main sofas tumbled backward, sending myself and the presenters flying across the studio floor.

I curled myself up in a ball and the light blast vanished. My hands tingled with heat, a spark every now and then shooting from each fingertip. I cautiously sat up, looking around

me in horror at the devastated studio.

Susannah Reid appeared from behind the upside-down sofa. Her hair was frazzling.

"Uh … thank you very much for joining us, Lightning Girl," she said, plastering a smile on her face as she directed her remarks toward a camera lying sideways on the floor, its red light still blinking. "We'll be right back after this quick break."

There was a knock on my door.

"Aurora?"

I heard the door open and Alexis's footsteps as he walked over to my bed. He prodded me gently through the duvet. I didn't respond, curling up tighter into a ball.

"Aurora," he said, nudging me again.

I still didn't say anything.

Nothing happened, so I thought he had given up and was leaving my room, but instead there was a long pause before my cozy duvet was yanked away from me.

"HEY!" I cried out, grappling to take it back as Alexis held it out of my reach triumphantly and then threw it to the other side of the room.

"You have to get out of bed. It's five p.m."

"Go away, Alexis," I grumbled, hugging my knees to my chest.

"You've spent two days hiding away in your room. You can't do the same today."

"It's none of your business. I can stay here all day if I want to. You shut yourself in your bedroom all the time and you LIVE in your smelly pajamas."

"Yeah, but I'm the eldest and a legend, so I can do whatever I want. Plus, I'm not hiding from anything like you are."

I frowned. "Give me back my duvet and leave me alone."

"Nope, not going to happen." He yawned,

checking his phone. "I'm not leaving this room until you're up."

I narrowed my eyes at him. "Why are you being so annoying?"

"Mostly because it's fun to annoy you. Your ears do this funny twitching thing when you're annoyed."

My hands flew to my ears. "They do not!"

"Yeah, they do. Why else do you think I always hide your shoes? Dad and I have a bet on about whether or not your ears will twitch when you come and ask us if we've seen them."

"WHAT? You and Dad have a bet about my ears? And I always thought it was Kimmy who was hiding my shoes!"

He shrugged. "Guilty."

"Ugh," I said, picking up my pillow and throwing it at him. "You are the WORST."

"But also a genius," he said, and grinned. "So, are you going to go take a shower or what? Because no offense, but you're not looking your best."

"Seriously, why did Mum send *you* to try and lure me out of my room?!" I asked. "You are not very good at this."

"Mum didn't send me. I took on this challenge myself out of the goodness of my heart."

I sighed. "Please can I have my duvet back? I'm freezing."

"No, you cannot. If you want to get warm, you'll have to get up and shower and then get dressed. Sorry," he shrugged, "those are my rules."

"Have you forgotten the time you stayed in your room for THREE DAYS? Dad had to leave meals outside your door!"

Alexis smiled smugly. "That was for a VERY

important project. I was hacking into some top secret software and every second mattered. You, on the other hand, are sulking."

"I'm not sulking," I muttered. "I'm just..."

"Feeling sorry for yourself?" He raised his eyebrows. "You almost destroyed a television studio and took out famous presenters live on air. So what? You should be used to embarrassing yourself by now. Have you met you?"

I threw my other pillow at him as he laughed at his HILARIOUS joke.

"Come on, Aurora," he coaxed. "It will blow over."

"It will NOT blow over. It hasn't blown over. Every time I go online, it's there, plastered across all the video channels with thousands of comments all about how I'm the worst superhero ever."

"Nah, not all of the comments say that."

I looked at him hopefully. "Really?"

"Sure. Some of the comments are about how bad you are at interviews. Oh and there's a couple about your hair. It didn't look its best after the light-beam explosion, to be fair. The frazzled look, if you will..."

"*ALEXIS!*"

"Who *cares* what people are saying?" He laughed, dodging the pen I threw at his head, now that I'd run out of pillows. "They don't know you. You shouldn't read those comments anyway."

My bedroom door swung open and Clara appeared in the doorway holding a stack of books.

"Hey, Mum and Dad mentioned you still won't leave your room," she said, coming in and plonking the pile onto my bedside table, knocking all my stuff off it in the process. "I thought these might cheer you up."

"*The Complete Guide to Physical and Theoretical Chemistry*," I said, reading the title on one of the spines aloud. "This is what you've brought to cheer me up?"

She blinked. "It works for me."

"Oh. Well. Thanks. I guess. That's very ... thoughtful of you, Clara."

She nodded and then glanced around my room before wrinkling her nose. "What's that smell?"

"That would be Aurora," Alexis answered gravely.

"I see."

"HEY! OK, FINE, I haven't had a shower today ... or yesterday ... but it is NOT that bad and you're both very annoying and PLEASE can you leave my room!" I instructed, pointing at the door. "Leave me to wallow in peace, ALONE!"

"Actually, psychological studies have

shown that isolation is unhealthy," Clara said matter-of-factly, climbing up onto my bed to sit cross-legged next to Alexis. "Perhaps you would like to discuss your feeling of failure?"

I buried my head in my hands. "WHY didn't I get NORMAL siblings?"

"Oh, yeah, *we're* the abnormal ones." Alexis snorted. "You literally shoot beams of light out of your hands."

He had a point. But, still.

"So," Clara prompted, "do you want to talk about it?"

I let out a long sigh. "Not really. There's not much to say. I let everyone down and now there's press surrounding my house, bothering my family, and I'm a total national embarrassment."

"International," Alexis corrected, winking at me.

I nodded glumly. "Right. International embarrassment. I don't deserve to be Lightning Girl."

"Says who?"

"Says the world, Alexis." I felt hot tears prickle behind my eyes. "Everyone thought I was someone I'm not. And now they've seen the truth."

Clara reached out and took my hand in her little one. "You're the best big sister in the world. That's who I think you are."

"Exactly," Alexis agreed, as I smiled gratefully at Clara. "You can't let yourself get down about what everyone else thinks of you. All that matters is what *I* think of you because, let's face it, I'm the most important person on the planet. And I think that there's obviously room for improvement, but when it comes down to it" – he grinned mischievously – "you're not too bad."

I giggled, wiping my eyes with my pajama sleeves.

"Hey," Alexis said, nudging Clara, "did she just laugh?"

"Yep, she DEFINITELY just laughed."

"Dad owes me five."

When I looked at him quizzically, Clara explained. "Alexis bet that he could make you laugh and leave your room by the end of the day. Dad thought you were too sad and you might need more space."

"I'm not sure I really had a choice about having some space for a bit longer," I commented, looking at them pointedly. "But, I'm a little bit glad you barged in. Just a little bit."

"I know you're upset, Aurora, but nobody thinks it's your fault," Clara said. "And Alexis promised that you could pick the film if you came downstairs for a family movie night."

"Did I?" He sighed. "Oh well, I'm a man of my word, so I guess I'll just go with it."

"Dad said we can have whatever you want for dinner," Clara continued. "And we won't talk about what happened unless you want to. So, will you come downstairs?"

I hesitated. "All right, then."

"Yes!" Alexis punched the air. "Dad owes me another five."

He jumped off the bed and went to leave the room.

"Oh, and not to rub it in or anything, sis," he said, as he got to the door, "but if you could bathe that would be great. Otherwise you'll have to sit in the dog bed with Kimmy for the movie. We don't want to have to spray the sofa afterward."

"He's only joking," Clara assured me as he disappeared down the stairs. "He may not show it, but he does have your back. Mum says he's been really worried about you."

"Yeah, yeah," I said dismissively, reaching for my laptop and pulling it up onto my knees.

"I'll go ask Mum and Dad to put on the popcorn," Clara said cheerily, sliding off the bed. "They'll be so pleased you're going to join us."

"Sounds good," I said, frowning at my computer screen as I refreshed the Internet page I'd been on. "Hey, that's weird."

"What is?" Clara asked, stopping in the doorway.

"I just went online to see how many YouTube views the video of me on *Good Morning Britain* has. I just tried refreshing the page, but it's not working. It just says content not available."

Clara watched me curiously as I typed my name into the search engine and scrolled down the results.

"I can't find the video anywhere," I told her in confusion. "It's just … disappeared from the Internet! How is this possible?!"

"It's like I said," Clara said, smiling knowingly. "Alexis has your back."

I stared openmouthed at her as she left the room. I tried finding the *Good Morning Britain* footage one last time on YouTube, but the same message appeared: *content unavailable.*

Grateful tears filled my eyes as I shut the lid of my laptop and swung my legs out of bed to head to the shower, suddenly feeling a little better than I did before.

I guess I'm OK with not having normal siblings, after all.

I woke up the next day to find an ostrich staring at me.

"Alfred!" I screamed, batting away his beak as he started pecking curiously at my pajamas. "When will you learn about personal space?"

Wearing denim dungarees, he strutted to the other side of the room to start rifling through my closet. I slumped back onto my pillows and pulled the duvet over my head. If Alfred was here, that only meant one thing.

"Aurora?" a voice trilled up the stairs. "Are you up?"

"No," I called back.

"Hello, darling!"

My bedroom door swung open and Aunt Lucinda stood in the frame, dressed head to toe in 1970s disco gear. Mum's twin sister was very eccentric in every possible way, including her fashion decisions and choice of sidekick.

None of us know why she decided on a grumpy, fashion-conscious pet ostrich, but they never went anywhere without each other. Despite his tendency to steal things and create mischief, Alfred had been key in stopping Mr. Mercury from getting away with the Light of the World, so I tried not to let it annoy me that he'd ripped up my bathrobe the last time he was here.

And I tried not to let it annoy me that he was currently pecking at the lenses of my new sunglasses.

And had now cracked them.

He threw them across the room in irritation and moved on to pecking at my desk.

"What are you still doing in bed?" Aunt Lucinda cried. "It's almost the evening!"

I looked at my phone. "It's ten a.m.!"

"Precisely," she said, sitting down on the edge of my bed. "Honestly, Aurora, I don't know why you felt it necessary to blow up the *Good Morning Britain* studio right in the middle of my vacation. Portugal really is fabulous this time of year and I had to cut my stay there short because of this whole palaver." She shook her head. "I only squeezed in four weeks there."

"Aren't you permanently on vacation?" I grumbled.

"I do try to be, my darling, but it's not as easy as you think, what with my niece causing chaos every five minutes. I felt that I simply had to be here to check in on you and make sure you're all right."

"Oh, really," I said, raising my eyebrows at her.

"Yes!" She lifted a hand to her heart dramatically. "How could you doubt my intentions?"

"Because last time you popped by, you said it was to support Dad on the grand opening of his big exhibition at the Natural History Museum, and it turned out that in fact you just wanted to steal the famous Dream Diamond from an auction house," I recalled, thinking about how she fooled me into helping her. "So, what's the real reason you and Alfred are here? I hope you're not planning on stealing the Crown Jewels again. There's a picture of you on a noticeboard outside the Tower of London so that the security team is sure not to let you in pretending to be a tourist."

"Really?" She patted her hair proudly. "I hope it's a good photograph."

I scowled at her. "Aunt Lucinda, I really have enough on my plate without you coming here and involving me in some kind of weird—"

"Honestly, Aurora," she said, standing up, "you sound more and more like my boring sister every day. Clearly, she's passed on that sensible gene to you. I am merely here to check on you … and if any of the paparazzi surrounding the house *happen* to take a picture of me looking fabulous, then that is a sacrifice I am willing to make."

"Ah." I smiled. "So, that's why you're here. For the fame."

"I don't know what you're talking about." She swanned toward the door. "Come along, Alfred, we can't keep Aurora's little friends waiting. They want to hear all about our trip to Fiji last month."

"Wait, what? What friends?"

"Didn't I mention them? Oh, that's why I came to wake you up. Your school friends are downstairs enjoying some hazelnut hot chocolate and droning on about the reporters that keep bothering them." She let out a long sigh. "I don't know why they're complaining. I'll see you downstairs."

She flounced out of the room and Alfred followed her, now wearing a pair of my shorts on his head as a hat. As his huge legs thumped down the stairs, I forced myself out of bed.

Since the *Good Morning Britain* disaster, the press had surrounded our house and refused to leave, desperate to try to get an interview with me or any kind of picture. The movie night with Alexis and Clara had been fun, but I still felt terrible about the whole thing. I just wanted to stay in bed until the end of summer vacation, by which time, hopefully, everyone would have forgotten I existed.

I got dressed and plodded downstairs, following the voices of the Bright Sparks coming from the kitchen. Dad was at the stove stirring a saucepan and Mum was standing on her tiptoes, getting the mugs down from the cupboard. Aunt Lucinda had taken a place at the table and was admiring her reflection in her pocket mirror, while Kimmy growled from her bed at Alfred pecking busily at the kitchen sink.

"Hey!" Kizzy beamed when she saw me. "How are you?"

"Have you seen the number of reporters outside your front door?" Suzie said, her eyes wide with wonder. "We had to literally push our way in!"

"It's awful, isn't it?" I grimaced. "I'm so sorry. It's not fair on anyone."

"No, Aurora, we're sorry too," Kizzy said gently, glancing guiltily at the others. "That's actually why we're here."

"We talked about it and we got a bit carried away in the excitement of it all," Georgie admitted as I looked at her in confusion. "We shouldn't have let you go on the show."

"You've had way too much on your shoulders," Fred added, crouching down to play with Kimmy and distract her from Alfred, who now had the salt shaker in his beak and was happily using it as a maraca, shaking salt all over the floor as he bopped to his own beat.

"Yeah. Obviously destroying one of the most famous studios in the country isn't brilliant—" Suzie began, receiving a sharp elbow in the ribs from Georgie. "Ouch! I was just saying that, although that's not great, your health is much more important."

Kizzy lifted her phone. "No more superhero schedule. I've cleared it all."

"We've all agreed that you need a break." Mum smiled cheerily as Dad nodded in agreement.

"Vacations are the key to success," Aunt Lucinda declared, snapping her mirror shut. "Right, I'm ready for my close-up with the press."

"But … I can't go on vacation," I said as Mum scowled at her sister. "We have the conference in a couple of weeks."

"You mean the very SECRET conference?" Aunt Lucinda asked, clearing her throat and looking pointedly at all my friends.

"Oh please. We've known about the secret Superhero Conference for weeks," Suzie said, folding her arms.

When one of the precious stones in Dad's exhibition turned out to be the Light of the World, superheroes across the world agreed that a secret conference was needed to determine its future because it was so precious and powerful. The conference had been arranged in London for this summer to discuss options, and only superheroes were invited.

Mum laughed at Aunt Lucinda's shocked expression. "They're heroes too, Lucinda. I felt that they deserved to know."

"If it wasn't for the Bright Sparks, I would have lost my job at the museum and the precious stones would have vanished," Dad said.

Georgie grinned. "Any time, Professor Beam."

"There's time for a trip before the Superhero Conference and I really think it would be a good idea for you to get away from all the madness and have a rest," Mum insisted, trying her best not to be distracted by Alfred.

He was now using the length of the kitchen as his catwalk, strutting back and forth with a saucepan on his head, wearing the dish towels as a different accessory each time.

His previous choice of headwear, my favorite shorts, had now been ripped in two and thrown impatiently across the room, hitting a confused Kimmy on the snout.

"So, where are you thinking?" Suzie asked excitedly. "Barbados?"

"The Maldives?" Georgie suggested.

"South of France?"

"The Bahamas?"

"Ah," Dad chuckled, "we were thinking of sending Aurora somewhere slightly more local."

"Dad can't get any time off from the museum at the moment, especially as he's already requested time off to come with us to the Superhero Conference," Mum explained apologetically. "You know that the summer is the busiest time of year in terms of tourists. And I need to stay in the UK in the lead-up to the conference, in case anyone tries to take over the world..."

"Casual reason." Kizzy laughed quietly.

"As neither of us can be with you," Mum continued, "we don't want to send you abroad on your own."

"OK." I nodded. "So, what's the plan?"

"The plan is for you to spend some time

in Cornwall," Dad announced.

"Cornwall?" Suzie looked at him, baffled. "What's in Cornwall?"

A mischievous smile spread across Aunt Lucinda's face. "Nanny Beam."

When I found out that all the Beam women were superheroes, I figured that Nanny Beam probably wasn't in Cornwall running a stray chicken sanctuary, like she said.

I thought that – just like Mum used to lie about being "at hot yoga" or "on a business trip" when she was in fact taking down villains – Nanny Beam had probably made up the whole chicken thing to cover her own flashy, superhero lifestyle.

I was wrong.

We see Nanny Beam once a year, but she always comes to visit us, so I didn't know what to expect as we trundled along the roads to her house in Cornwall. Aunt Lucinda had insisted on joining us for the drive because she was considering buying an island off the coast of Cornwall and decided Mum could drop her off at the port afterward.

"You're not driving? What happened to your cool sports car?" Fred had asked Aunt Lucinda as the Bright Sparks helped me pack my suitcase.

"It's a long story," she'd said with a sigh, taking a sip from a cocktail. "It involves an ill-advised bet and a mountain. I'll tell you all about it another time."

She was sitting in the front seat next to Mum, so I was stuck in the back with Alfred, pushing his silly feathers away from my face for the entire journey. To fit in the car, he had to have the window down and stick his neck out the whole time, otherwise he got a neck cramp. And according to Aunt Lucinda, an ostrich with a neck cramp is terrible company. He was wearing special military pilot goggles so that his eyes wouldn't water when we sped along.

After hours of me being incredibly cold and uncomfortable squished in next to an ostrich, we turned off the busy road and were soon driving down deserted country lanes and through beautiful rolling green hills. Alfred pecked loudly on the roof of the car to alert us that he had spotted the sea.

"Where are we going?" I asked, as we cruised along the coastline, seemingly getting farther from civilization and nearer to the edge of the cliffs. "Is Nanny Beam some kind of mermaid?"

"Very funny." Mum chuckled, although considering our family's history, I wouldn't have been that surprised if it had been true. "Her house is a bit isolated. It's beautiful; just you wait."

We turned a corner and Mum nodded ahead of us. "There."

Perched right on a cliff edge was a lovely little cottage, surrounded by what looked like lots of wooden huts and stables. A mixture of horses, donkeys, llamas, goats and sheep were dotted around the fields, grazing peacefully. It looked exactly like a postcard.

"Wow," I gasped, staring at it in awe.

"She has expanded her chicken sanctuary. She now runs a rescue home for any and all stray animals," Mum explained, parking in front of the house.

I climbed out of the car, listening to the waves crash onto the cliff below, breathing in the fresh air. It felt as though there was no one else around for miles. Alfred, who had untangled his neck from the window, squeezed out of the car bottom-first, before wobbling onto the front lawn to begin some stretches, starting with the splits.

"He does hate long journeys, poor thing. Legroom is always a problem when traveling with an ostrich," Aunt Lucinda noted. "And of course, normally we travel first class…"

Mum rolled her eyes as she got out of the car and rubbed her neck. "I'm so sorry. His

Majesty can get a lift with someone else if he'd rather."

Aunt Lucinda opened her mouth to reply, but before she could, the front door of the cottage swung open and the first thing I saw was a shock of bright-pink hair.

"Welcome! Welcome!" Nanny Beam exclaimed, hurrying down the front steps with her arms outstretched.

She pulled me in for a big hug, enveloping me in the flowing multicolored poncho she was wearing. Dad had always said it would be wonderful to have a competition to work out who was more bonkers: Nanny Beam or Aunt Lucinda. But then he'd always receive a very sharp look from Mum and change the subject.

"Cool hair, Nanny Beam!" I laughed, admiring the color. "Last time I saw you, it was blue."

"Ah yes," she tutted, shaking her head. "Luckily, I grew out of that phase. I am so excited to have you here." She smiled. "We're going to have a lovely, relaxing time. I've got some marvelous exercises up my sleeve, which is just what you need."

"Exercises?" Mum asked curiously, coming over to greet her. "I specifically said no superpower training. Aurora needs a break."

"Don't be so ridiculous, Kiyana," Nanny Beam said, throwing an arm over my shoulders. "I'm talking yoga, meditation, everything Aurora needs right now. For example, I... WAIT! STOP!"

We all froze.

"What?" Mum said in a panic, her eyes darting all around. "What is it?"

Aunt Lucinda waved her arms frantically. "Is it a bee? Where? WHERE?"

"Shush! Listen! Feel it!" Nanny Beam

pointed at the sun, closed her eyes and inhaled deeply. "Can you feel that, Aurora? Can you?"

"Uh." I looked to Mum for help, but she just shrugged. "What am I supposed to be feeling? What's going on?"

"Don't worry," Nanny Beam said, opening her eyes and exhaling. "It's called Sun Gazing. By the end of the week you'll have a knack for it! It will help your soul to blossom and regenerate your light within."

"Sun Gazing? Oh for goodness' sake, Mummy," Aunt Lucinda hissed. "You almost gave me a heart attack. I thought it was a bee! I must have aged about five years. I'll start looking the same age as Kiyana!"

Mum narrowed her eyes at her. "We're *twins*."

"Always bickering, you two. I bet you were arguing in the womb. Come on," Nanny Beam said, chuckling. "Let's get inside and I'll show Aurora to her room. Then I need to feed the alpacas."

"How are all the alpacas?" Mum asked, helping me bring in my bags, while Aunt Lucinda checked in her mirror for any new wrinkles that may have formed on her face in the past two minutes.

"Marvelous, of course! Although, Augusta is being a bit off with me today, but I think that's because I accidentally tripped over her foot earlier. But, really, she shouldn't have been Sun Gazing on the roof. Of course, I was going to trip over her there. Do you like alpacas, Aurora?"

She rambled on about the alpacas the whole time she showed me to my room. Her cottage was as beautiful on the inside as it was from the outside. The ceilings were low, with old wooden beams across them, and the floorboards creaked under your foot. There were framed photographs of us all dotted about everywhere, and chickens were wandering about the house freely, strolling in from the garden to see what was going on inside.

Coming up the stairs, I heard a loud bang behind me as Alfred knocked his head on a beam and then angrily pecked at it in revenge.

"Don't bring the house down, darling," Aunt Lucinda warned him, giving him a comforting pet.

He marched huffily back down the stairs and went to have a staring contest with a cockerel.

"This is your room," Nanny Beam said proudly, standing aside to let me in. "Do you like it?"

It was a lovely bedroom, with pale-blue walls and a vase of sunflowers next to the bed. I strolled over to the window and looked out.

I could see for miles across the green fields and the sparkling blue sea. I already felt a lot more relaxed.

"It's perfect."

Nanny Beam clapped her hands together and then invited us all down for a cup of tea before Mum and Aunt Lucinda carried on with their journey.

"Will you be all right for the week here?" Mum asked me before she left.

Aunt Lucinda was in the front of the car waiting and Alfred was strewn across the back seat, flicking through a book Nanny Beam had lent him on the history of animal rights.

"Yes, of course. I think this was a really good idea," I admitted.

"Me too. Have a wonderful time." Mum smiled, pulling me in for one last hug. "You'll be relaxed and refreshed before the Superhero Conference."

She straightened and turned to face Nanny Beam. "Thanks, Mum, and remember" – she gave her a stern look – "no trouble."

"Oh, Kiyana," Nanny Beam said, putting an arm round my shoulder and waving goodbye, "what trouble could possibly happen here?"

7

I woke up the next day and lay in bed, feeling confused.

Nobody was shaking me awake, telling me I was late for something. There were no frantic messages on my phone about lost pets or household tasks where my help was urgently needed. No alarm clock was going off. I wasn't required to be anywhere or do anything.

It was so … *nice*.

I stretched my arms and sat up to reach over to the window and draw the curtains. Sunlight poured in, making me squint. I peered out at the beautiful view, enjoying the warmth on my face and the tranquil sound of gentle waves.

Suddenly, my bedroom door swung open.

"Good morning, Aurora!" Nanny Beam trilled, coming in with a cup of tea and several chickens who trotted into the bedroom alongside her. "I was just outside feeding the birds and saw your face at the window. How did you sleep?"

Today she was wearing several beaded necklaces over her green top and brightly patterned trousers that were so floaty that I thought it was a long skirt at first.

She'd tied her pink hair back with a thin purple scarf that had silver tassels at the end and was hanging down her back. She looked as though she was about to step into a time machine and attend a music festival in the 1960s. She looked wonderful.

"I slept really well." I smiled, thanking her for the tea as she placed the mug on my bedside table before sitting on the edge of the bed. "I feel like I'm actually on summer vacation here."

"Good," Nanny Beam said, clapping her hands enthusiastically and giving one of the chickens a bit of a fright. She clucked indignantly. "It's a beautiful day, so we can have a lovely stroll down to the beach if you like. The chickens could do with stretching their legs, as could the alpacas. And the horses. And donkeys. Well, everyone, I suppose. What do you think, girls?" she asked, addressing the chickens strutting around the room. "Shall we have a day at the beach?"

They clucked in excitement, making me giggle.

"Wonderful creatures, chickens," Nanny Beam said.

"I like them a lot." I smiled, sipping my tea as a chicken began nuzzling Nanny Beam's ankle. "Have you always loved animals?"

"Oh, yes. I always thought I was going to be a vet, but then when I found out about the superpowers, I realized that I was bound to a different path." She sighed. "My bizarre connection with animals suddenly made sense."

I looked at her in confusion. "What does that have to do with your powers?"

"Didn't Kiyana tell you? That's my extra power, if you will," she explained, her bright-green eyes twinkling. "Just as your mum is incredibly fast and Lucinda has powers of persuasion and charm, I have a rather extraordinary bond with animals. I feel very lucky. That's why I started the sanctuary when I retired from saving the world. I knew it was my destiny to provide a home to any animals who were in need."

"That's so cool. I don't know what my extra power is yet."

"Don't you?" Nanny Beam asked curiously. "I should have thought yours was the strongest of all. Especially considering your powers have appeared at so young an age."

"Yes, but that's just because the Light of the World was found again, so it brought my powers into play earlier than normal. It has nothing to do with me."

Nanny Beam's eyes flickered toward the swirled scar on my palm, before lifting her gaze to meet mine and a wide smile crept across her face.

"I wouldn't be too sure about that, Aurora

Beam. I think you're very special. Don't you worry, we'll find out your extra power soon enough. Anyway" – she abruptly stood up, causing all the chickens to stop what they were doing and stand to attention in a military row – "let's not waste this beautiful sunshine! When you're ready, Aurora, we shall all have a lovely outing. I'll let the others know what the plan is. I imagine Augusta the alpaca will have something negative to say about it. She loves to cause drama, that one."

She rolled her eyes and then swanned out of the room, the trail of chickens following her eagerly.

Over the next few days I fell into a routine with Nanny Beam and her wacky life. Every morning I'd help her feed the many animals before we would all walk to the top of the cliff for a yoga lesson in the sunshine. I had never done yoga before, but Nanny Beam helped me. I loved it, even though I wasn't very flexible and occasionally tumbled over onto my bottom, making the donkeys bray with laughter. Chickens, it turns out, are very good at yoga.

"Lucinda's ostrich, Alfred, loves yoga and Pilates," Nanny Beam informed me as we made our way back to the cottage one morning. "I've learned a lot from him."

I spent the afternoons reading books on the beach or playing in the sea with the donkeys before heading home to tuck into a delicious healthy dinner. I felt very sophisticated, as though I was on one of those posh retreats that Hollywood actors like to do.

When it got to my last day, I felt sad that I was leaving.

"Me too, Aurora," Nanny Beam said gently, when I told her so. "In fact, I feel so down about it, I'm going to go sit on the roof."

Although that might cause most grandchildren to worry, Nanny Beam announcing that she was heading to the roof was part of her daily routine. She would sit, meditating and Sun Gazing and getting cross with any alpacas that she tripped over up there.

"Augusta!" I heard her yell. "Stop eating the tiles!"

While Nanny Beam was on the roof, I decided to take my book and read in the sitting room until she came down. Before I got curled up in the armchair, I took a moment to admire all her photos and trinkets on the mantelpiece. She'd told me that all the bits and bobs in here were collected from her previous adventures around the world. There were several wooden and marble carvings, a delicate ancient fan and an intricate music box.

I opened the music box and it began to play a soft tinkling melody. In the middle of the box, spinning to the music, was a tiny model of a ballet-dancing chicken. I giggled, rolling my eyes. Trust Nanny Beam to have found a *chicken* music box. Wondering where in the world she got it from, I reached forward and touched the top of the chicken's head to get a closer look.

I must have pressed it a bit harder than I meant to. There was a sharp clicking sound as the chicken was pushed down, like I had accidentally pressed a button. The music box came to a sudden halt.

I began freaking out that I had broken something very precious before a series of loud clunking noises started coming from underneath the mantelpiece. A loud boom echoed round the room and the fireplace swung open, revealing a dimly lit metal staircase behind it.

It wasn't a fireplace at all. It was a secret door.

"What on earth?" I whispered, crouching

to peer inside.

I glanced back at the empty room. Nanny Beam must still have been on the roof and I was much too curious not to see what was down there.

Wishing the Bright Sparks were here with me – Fred would have LOVED this – I ducked through the fireplace and crept carefully down the steps. It was pitch-black at the bottom and I tried to feel along the walls, but I couldn't find a light switch anywhere.

I held my hands out.

Since arriving at Nanny Beam's a week ago, I hadn't used my superpowers. Not just because I was here on vacation and taking a break from it all, but also because I was terrified after causing such havoc on *Good Morning Britain*. I hadn't felt in control at all and I could have hurt someone. All my confidence had fizzled away after the incident and just the idea of using them was making my hands shake.

"Come on, Aurora," I whispered to myself through the darkness. "You can do this."

I closed my eyes and took a deep breath, pulling all my focus to my powers. At first nothing happened, but then I began to feel that strange tingling feeling and a couple of bright sparks burst out of my fingertips. With all the energy I could find, I began to produce a very dim glow from my palms, not nearly as sparkling or bright as normal.

But I guess it was a start.

Using my faint glimmer, I was able to make out that I was in a large underground space. I could just see the outline of some dark shapes, but I couldn't see what they were without getting closer.

I took a step forward and bright strip lights automatically flickered on in the ceiling, right across the room. As my eyes got used to the light, I was able to make out what all those shapes were.

My breath caught in my throat.

Computers. Loads of them; really high-

tech ones too, with the biggest screens I'd ever seen, and glass cases dotted along the side containing weird-looking gadgets. The vast room was shiny, minimalist and modern, with steel silver walls, no windows and a huge control panel of different colored buttons right in front of me. It was like wandering into the gadget scene of a James Bond film or a flashy spaceship movie. Alexis would have been in heaven here.

I gazed across the room in shock, my mouth hanging open.

What was this place?

A cough came from behind me, making me jump out of my skin.

I spun round to see Nanny Beam watching me from the bottom of the stairs.

"Hello, Aurora," she said, a mischievous grin spreading across her face. "I see you've discovered my little secret."

"N ... Nanny Beam" – I stammered – "what is all this?"

She let out a long sigh and stepped forward to stand right in front of me.

"Aurora, I will tell you. But I need you to promise me that you won't repeat it to a soul. Do you promise?"

I glanced nervously at all the computer screens and then looked back to her. She bent down to look closely into my eyes.

"Promise?"

I gulped before nodding vigorously. "I promise."

"All right then."

She stood up straight and turned on her heel to face a small flat silver panel in the wall. She cleared her throat.

"Activate," she said clearly.

A red light came on in the middle of the panel, projecting a thin line across her forehead that scanned down to her chin and disappeared.

"Facial and retinal recognition," she explained, turning to look over her shoulder at me as the light blinked from red to green. "It's the latest model."

"Welcome, Patricia," a computerized voice greeted her, with surround sound booming throughout the room.

"Thank you," she replied to the panel in the wall. "Turn on all systems, please."

"Turning on all systems."

A whirring sound echoed through the basement as the dozens of computers came to life. All of them seemed to display something different. Some turned on random security footage, each screen flicking every few seconds to a different scene, while other screens flashed up lines of continuously scrolling green data: jumbled letters and numbers, which didn't make any sense.

Nanny Beam chuckled as she witnessed my reaction. My mouth had become very dry from hanging open so long.

I was in complete and utter SHOCK. My *grandmother,* who everyone thought was a sweet, slightly bonkers, retired old lady, had a SECRET UNDERGROUND LAIR. My grandmother! Nanny Beam! Who likes talking to chickens and alpacas! HAS AN UNDERGROUND LAIR. WITH A HIGH-TECH LASER SECURITY SYSTEM.

WHAT IS HAPPENING?

"I've always been fascinated by technology," Nanny Beam said fondly, as my brain became as scrambled as the rolling data on the screens surrounding me. "Much like Alexis. I think he got that streak from me."

"I ... I..."

I tried to form words, but I was too stunned by the madness of it all. Nanny Beam has bright-pink hair and does yoga on the rooftop. Grannies with bright-pink hair and hundreds of aromatherapy candles do NOT have these kind of secret spy bunkers filled with the latest technology built underneath their quaint seaside cottages.

Do they?

"The truth is," Nanny Beam began, watching my mouth silently open and close like a fish, "I was never able to give the superhero thing up completely. I tried to retire from the life and take a step back, but it was a lot harder to leave it behind than I thought it would be. The Beam women have always been on hand to save the world, which is tricky enough, but nobody ever tells you the most difficult part of the job."

"Letting go?" I managed to croak eventually.

"Actually, it's letting your *daughter* go," she corrected gently, avoiding eye contact. "Every Beam woman has to step aside and then watch her daughter devote her life to stopping danger." She let out a long sigh. "I have never stopped being sick with worry at Kiyana putting herself in harm's way to save the world. She's a fantastic superhero, your mum, but in my eyes, she'll always be my little girl."

"Wait a moment," I said, holding up my hands. "Let me get this straight. You've been secretly saving the world too, all this time? You weren't running an animal sanctuary after all?"

"No, no, no, don't be so ridiculous, Aurora." She laughed, although it didn't seem at all ridiculous to me considering we were standing in the middle of her SECRET UNDERGROUND LAIR. "Of course, I'm running my animal sanctuary. I merely like to keep an eye on things. And be available for backup, just in case. Kiyana has no idea about all this."

Nanny Beam held out her palms and made them glow with a neon pink sparkling light. She grinned, wiggling her fingers. "There's still life in me yet."

"But Nanny Beam, Mum would kill you if she knew," I said, walking over to a computer screen that was showing a debate going on in the House of Commons. "You're supposed to be living a quiet life, saving chickens!"

She shrugged. "That's why I made you

promise to keep it secret. This is all just a bit of fun."

"Then the wacky, hippie thing you have going on is all just an act? A front to hide the fact that you're actually a *serious technological mastermind*?"

She furrowed her brow in confusion. "What wacky, hippie thing?"

"Uh … nothing. Never mind," I said hurriedly, changing the subject. "Does Mum have something like this, too? She's never shown me her secret superhero headquarters. Is it under our house?"

"No, I don't think so," Nanny Beam chuckled. "Kiyana is a bit more of a hands-on superhero. She's never been one for computers."

I ran my eyes over a big control panel, which had hundreds of buttons and then one big red one in the middle. "What happens if you press that?"

"Everything self-destructs in five seconds."

I instinctively jumped backward before Nanny Beam burst out laughing.

"You're joking, right?" I said hopefully.

She grinned. "I guess you'll never know. I shall have to be extra careful around you, now that I know you have a prominent curious streak. There I was thinking that the music box was a stroke of genius. Who would guess that the dancing chicken is a button? I'll have to think of something else and get that sorted."

"You don't even have a computer in the cottage," I said, still wondering if I was in some kind of weird dream.

Nanny Beam watched as I wandered along the first row of computers, examining the footage on the screens. Suddenly, one of the computers started making a beeping sound. Nanny Beam hurried over to it and peered at the monitor.

"Ah," she said. "I just need to make a quick business phone call, Aurora. I won't be a moment. Stay right there and then I'll give you the full tour."

She marched to the opposite side of the room, before lifting her wrist to her mouth, appearing to speak into her bracelet. I shook my head and continued to admire all the gadgets.

There was a large pile of backdated folders on one of the desks near me which looked out of place among all this high-tech equipment – clearly Nanny Beam's filing system from a long time ago. I didn't think much of the stack of crumpled paper and files until I noticed an old photograph sticking out of them.

I pulled out the picture to look at it more closely. It was Nanny Beam from a long time ago standing next to a man and a boy, neither of whom I recognized. I squinted closely at the man and smiled when I realized that he had exactly the same nose and curious expression as Nanny Beam – this must be her brother. Mum had mentioned her uncle a couple of times, but it was an uncomfortable topic for her because, apparently, he and Nanny Beam had had a major falling out before he passed away when Mum was a teenager. After that, Nanny Beam never talked about him. It was nice to see what he had looked like.

I heard her footsteps coming back and quickly pushed the photo back into the file, not wanting to upset her. As I did, an old newspaper clipping slipped out and fluttered to the floor. I quickly bent to pick it up.

"What's that?" she asked curiously as I straightened.

"Oh, it … it just fell out from your file."

As I held it out to her, I caught a glance of the headline: *LIGHT EXPLOSION IN WAREHOUSE!*

"Whoa." I grimaced. "That doesn't sound good."

"It wasn't," she said gravely, glancing at the clipping and then placing it carefully onto the desk. She gestured toward the files with a wave of her hand. "These are just all old cases of mine, back when I was doing your mother's job. So" – her expression softened – "what do you think of it?"

"You mean, your underground lair? I can't get my head round this place! It's just so ... *cool*. I feel like I'm in a movie."

"You haven't even seen the best bit," she said excitedly, gesturing for me to follow her. "I have to say, although it's not ideal that you happened upon my secret, it is quite fun to be able to share it with someone. I've never been able to show it off before. Come on, this way."

I followed her to the back of the room, past the glass cabinets containing random objects, which Nanny Beam explained to me on the way. For example, glittering silver, heart-shaped sunglasses – *"they can shoot out laser beams"*; an orange feather boa – *"that transforms into a zip line at the press of a button. Very handy when stuck on a roof"*; a stickered skateboard – *"powered with a built-in jet engine, so goes extremely fast. Last time I used it, I got terrible windburn on my cheeks"*; and a microphone – *"you'd be surprised at how many evil geniuses out there have a soft spot for karaoke. Offer them a moment in the spotlight before they begin their evil plans and they simply can't resist taking the mic to belt out a ballad. But that microphone morphs into unbreakable handcuffs, trapping you as soon as you hold it."*

"Do you develop all these gadgets yourself?" I asked in awe.

"No, I have contacts. Although the microphone was my idea," she said proudly, as I shook my head in disbelief. "Rather pleased with that one. It's used all over the world."

We stopped as we got to the back of the room, the wall there being a large mirror like the ones in dance studios. It made the room feel like it went on forever and ever. Nanny Beam stepped sideways to face another silver panel, this one embedded into the mirror.

"Activate."

Her face was once again scanned, but after the light went green, she pressed her thumb onto the panel too.

"Fingerprint authentication," she explained, winking at me.

"Password," the computerized voice demanded.

"Silkie-Orpington-Leghorn." She smiled at my confused expression, adding: "All types of chicken breeds. Marvelous creatures. I change the password every day, of course. Extra security measures needed for this end of the room."

"Nanny Beam." I gulped. "What is behind this mirror?"

"You'll see!" she replied enthusiastically.

There was a loud clunking sound as the mirror began to slide up into the ceiling. Nanny Beam was practically shaking with excitement next to me, muttering under her breath, "Oh, I can't wait for you to see! *I can't wait for you to see!*"

As the bottom of the mirror wall rose high above my head, revealing the space concealed behind it, Nanny Beam whispered dreamily, "What do you think? Isn't she *magnificent*?"

Sitting on a launchpad was a wide, streamlined, neon-pink, shiny, futuristic sports car. It was the most amazing car I had EVER seen.

Nanny Beam clapped her hands, swooning at the mere sight of it, before launching into a list of its hidden features.

"An engine more powerful than turbine jets;

lighter than a feather; the fastest car *in the world*; invisibility feature, of course; fireproof, flood proof and bulletproof; extremely spacious inside. I've been able to fit a couple of the alpacas in the back seat, would you believe? Laser light beams; fully decked-out computer system; cameras on every corner; AND," she paused, inhaling dramatically, "she can *fly*."

"It … it can fly?"

"*She*, Aurora. Not it. She has feelings,"

Nanny Beam scolded. "And yes. She can fly. That's a new feature I'm yet to test out. I think I'll give her a couple more checks before I try to get her in the air, but I imagine she will be ready for that in a week or so."

We stood in silence for ages staring at the car before Nanny Beam turned to look at me.

"What do you think?" she asked eagerly.

"I think…" I began, a dazed smile spreading across my face, "I think that it is safe to say you are the coolest granny on the planet."

Nanny Beam put an arm round my shoulders, pulling me close.

"So, if you promise you won't tell your mother," she said, her eyes twinkling, "how do you feel about taking her for a spin?"

Mum stopped in front of a lamppost.

"Here we are!" she announced brightly, pushing her sunglasses up her nose.

Dad and I shared a look.

"Um, Mum?" I said, as Dad tried and failed to suppress a snigger. "That's a lamppost."

"Yes. And?"

"And we're supposed to be going to the Superhero Conference."

"Exactly." Mum nodded.

"I think I had better get you some water,

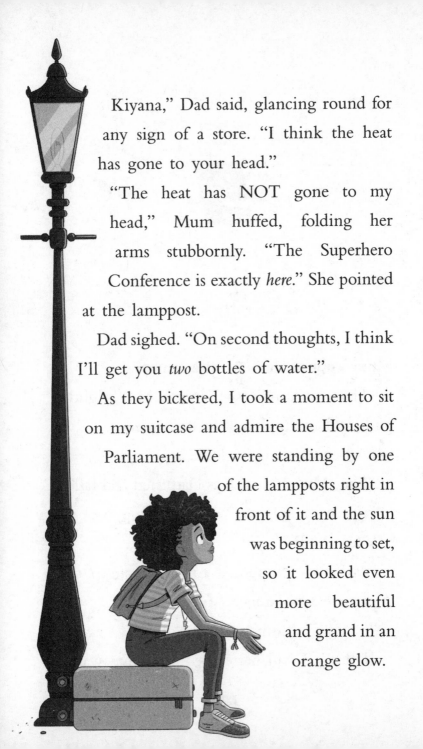

Kiyana," Dad said, glancing round for any sign of a store. "I think the heat has gone to your head."

"The heat has NOT gone to my head," Mum huffed, folding her arms stubbornly. "The Superhero Conference is exactly *here*." She pointed at the lamppost.

Dad sighed. "On second thoughts, I think I'll get you *two* bottles of water."

As they bickered, I took a moment to sit on my suitcase and admire the Houses of Parliament. We were standing by one of the lampposts right in front of it and the sun was beginning to set, so it looked even more beautiful and grand in an orange glow.

I felt excited about the conference, but apprehensive too. I didn't really know what to expect and even though I had been asking Mum loads of questions about it since I got back from Nanny Beam's, she hadn't been very helpful.

"The last Superhero Conference like this one was *years* ago, Aurora," she'd said in a tired voice when I asked her about it for the twentieth time that day. "I can't really remember all the details, but it was just lots of superheroes in a room having a big discussion. Boring really."

Except this time it surely *wouldn't* be boring, especially since the whole reason for the conference was because we had found the most precious stone in existence, the Light of the World, and needed to decide where it would be safe. And it DEFINITELY wouldn't be boring for me because that stone is the source of all my superpowers.

Anyway, when Mum said that we were going to the Houses of Parliament for the Superhero Conference, Dad and I got really excited because I'd never been there before, and Dad always gets excited about geeky stuff like old buildings.

Clara was very jealous that she wasn't allowed to come with us.

"Have fun," she'd said glumly when we'd waved goodbye this morning. "Try and appreciate the perpendicular Gothic style of the Palace of Westminster."

"We're not going to the Palace of Westminster," I'd corrected, smiling at my little sister. "We're going to the Houses of Parliament."

She'd let out a long sigh and plodded up the

stairs with a new encyclopedia tucked under her arm. "The Palace of Westminster *is* the Houses of Parliament, Aurora."

Kizzy had been equally as jealous when I told her on the phone where we were going, making me promise to take some photos. I had missed the Bright Sparks loads while I had been away in Cornwall and was hoping to see them before leaving for the conference, but they were all on their own summer vacations with their families.

I WISHED I could tell them all about Nanny Beam's secret lair and her supercar; it took all my self-control not to let such cool information slip out. Driving around the country lanes of Cornwall with Nanny Beam had been like zooming around in a luxurious space rocket.

They had all messaged me to say good luck for the conference on our group chat: Georgie had reminded me to bring my special new Lightning Girl jacket, Suzie had told me to practice my cartwheels during any free time I had as they needed "a LOT of work," and Kizzy promised to organize a Bright Sparks meeting when I returned. Fred said good luck too and then informed us that he believed he'd just broken the loudest burp world record and his mum had banished him from the room because of his achievement.

"Henry, for the last time, I do NOT need any water," Mum hissed, as Dad continued to outline the symptoms of dehydration. "This lamppost is the entrance to the conference. When has my sense of direction ever let us down before?"

Dad harrumphed and muttered under his breath, "How long have you got?"

Mum ignored him and inspected the lamppost closely. "This is definitely it. Look at all the other lampposts on this road. What's different about this one?"

I glanced up and down at the tall, elegant, black lampposts lining the pavement around the Houses of Parliament. Then I looked back at the one Mum was standing next to.

"This one isn't on and all the others are?" I suggested.

"Exactly! The reason it isn't on is because it's not really a lamppost; it's a door."

I shrugged at Dad as Mum checked to make sure there weren't any tourists or busy Londoners looking our way, before crouching to pretend to tie her shoelace. Instead, she pressed something at the bottom of the lamppost and then stood up straight.

"Kiyana Beam! It's been years!"

We jumped at the shrill voice that suddenly came from behind us, turning to see a tall dark-haired woman wearing blue lipstick and a long blue summer dress. She held out her arms and drew Mum into a big hug.

"Crystal!" Mum grinned, hugging her back. "How are you?"

"Very pleased to see you! I think the last time I saw you was that boring conference about that volcano. You remember, when the lava was green, and everyone went mad thinking the world was ending? Turned out to be a villain, who you managed to sort out in five seconds flat! You always were one of the best." She turned to smile at me and Dad. "This must be your handsome husband and charming daughter!"

Dad blushed all the way to his roots and mumbled something incoherent as she shook his hand.

"Almost everyone is here now. You had better go in or else Mr. Vermore will start getting twitchy. He's very strict about the conference running on schedule and is bossing us all about, despite the fact that he has no superpowers to speak of. I honestly think if he's not careful, Benjamin Jackson – you know, the very strong, handsome hero from Lagos – is going to lose his temper."

The name Vermore rang a bell, but I couldn't work out why.

"Right," Crystal said, clapping her hands. "Let's open the door, shall we? But first I just need to sort the safety measures. If you could all stand very still on those four paving slabs. Don't forget your luggage. I'll see you soon; I just have to wait for the remaining guests to arrive and then I'll be joining you all."

Mum, Dad and I did as she instructed, stepping onto the indicated squares around the lamppost. She winked at Mum and then inhaled deeply, wiggling her fingers. I gasped as a thin sparkling blue bubble seemed to form around us and the lamppost.

"Crystal has invisibility superpowers," Mum informed me, watching her in admiration. "She can create an invisible field and a hallucination around us. Nobody on the street can see us now. All they see is the lamppost and the pavement exactly how it should be. She can't do it for very long, but it is quite an amazing superpower."

Suddenly, the paving slabs began to lower through the pavement. I gripped on to Mum's arm as we sank into the ground, passersby not noticing a thing. Crystal waved cheerfully to us from the street. The pavement slabs came to a halt, level with the doors of a large transparent pod with seats inside.

We stepped off and into the glass pod and the pavement gradually went back up, closing above us.

"Sit down," Mum said, excitedly. "And

you'll need to put on your seat belt."

Dad and I nervously buckled into our seats. Before I had time to ask Mum what was about to happen, the glass bubble jolted forward, speeding through a tunnel, turning and twisting, making my stomach drop, before coming to a sudden halt. It opened its doors onto a platform, and I felt a bit dizzy as I stood up, as though I'd just been on a roller coaster.

"Isn't that a fun way of getting around! The Superhero Express!" Mum exclaimed, dragging our luggage out. Dad didn't look like he'd had much fun. He had gone very green and Mum had to go back into the pod to help him undo his seat belt.

"The Beams! Welcome!"

A burly man with thick dark hair and strong eyebrows, wearing an expensive-looking suit, came hurrying over to greet us, holding out his hand to Mum.

"What an honor to meet you. I'm Darek Vermore," he said, beaming at me. "You may know my tagline: *Vermore, for those who want more.*"

I realized why I had recognized the name Vermore before. He was a powerful businessman, who ran loads of big London tech companies. Alexis worshipped him, and I'd seen his ads on television, where he'd say the tagline at the end with a cheesy smile.

But as I shook his hand, something niggled at the back of my brain. As though I'd seen him somewhere else, other than on his ads. I just couldn't place him.

"Of course, I know who you are," Mum said as she smiled warmly. "Thank you for

providing all the technology and equipment we need for the next few days."

"Not at all. Sponsoring the Superhero Conference is an honor. I'm extremely proud of this building and my company's advanced security technology," he added, in a more serious tone. "Rest assured, Mrs. Beam, the Light of the World will be safe here. I assume you have it with you? How exciting."

His wide eyes flickered toward her handbag. Mum's hand drifted over it protectively.

Vermore opened his mouth to say something but was interrupted by a short man with thick-rimmed glasses and scruffy blond hair. The new arrival came running over to us, tripping over his feet and landing flat on his face, sending the computer tablet he was holding scattering across the platform. He looked as though he belonged in a cartoon.

I quickly bent down to get the tablet as Mum and Dad, who had now recovered from the Superhero Express, helped him up.

"Are you all right?" Mum asked, handing him his glasses.

"Aye, I'm so sorry, so sorry. Thank you, thank you," he spluttered in a thick Scottish accent, as I gave him the tablet back. "That was lucky! It didn't crack!"

Mr. Vermore was looking at him with disgust and I immediately felt sorry for whoever he was.

"Ah yes, this is my new assistant." Mr. Vermore sighed impatiently, as though annoyed that he had to take the time to introduce him. "David Donnelly. He's yet to get the hang of things, so I'm afraid you'll have to be *very* patient with him."

"Are there any refreshments I can get you?" David asked quietly, so embarrassed he hardly dared to look at us.

"I'm all right, thank you, David. That's very kind of you," Mum said kindly, shooting a glare at Mr. Vermore who was too busy flicking a speck of dust from his pocket square to notice.

"I think it's time you showed the Beams to their rooms," Mr. Vermore snarled at David. "Help them with their bags."

David nodded and beckoned us to follow him along the platform to the large doors at the end.

"Relax and settle in, Beams," Mr. Vermore called out behind us, his booming voice echoing around the platform. "And then the real fun can begin!"

10

"WOW!"

I had to rub my eyes to believe what I was seeing. Twice.

The Superhero Conference was the coolest place EVER. When David opened the doors from the platform, I wasn't sure what to expect, but I wasn't expecting to step forward into a HUGE, spectacular glass dome. It was so high, I had to squint my eyes to see the top of the curved ceiling.

There were several large metallic circular

doors around the dome and I watched in awe as someone walked up to one, pressed a button at its side and the metal door opened in a spiral. The vast central space of the dome was split into sections – there was a seating area around a beautiful fountain where people were lounging, drinking coffee and chatting; and on the other side of the dome was what looked like a small overgrown jungle, with trees, plants and colorful flowers. Someone was taking a nap in a hammock in the middle of it.

"I can't believe this is right below the Houses of Parliament, built so far underground," Dad said, polishing his glasses with his shirt before putting them back on to make sure he was seeing things correctly. "Outstanding architecture. I'd love to learn more about it."

"I have pamphlets," David said hurriedly, checking his pockets. "Argh, I must have left them somewhere. Mr. Vermore is going to *kill* me if I've lost them."

"It's all right," Dad assured him warmly. "You can just let me know when and if you find them."

"It's weird, isn't it?" Mum smiled, enjoying my stunned reaction. "Would you believe, Aurora, that such an underground complex exists where you'd never expect?"

Actually, I thought, *I can completely believe that, because my grandmother happens to have one of her own, built underneath her quaint Cornwall cottage.*

But I obviously couldn't say that out loud.

"It's amazing," I said instead. "Is everyone in here a superhero?"

"Oh yes," David nodded. "Everyone except me. And Mr. Vermore, of course."

As if on cue, one of the women lounging next to the fountain began to entertain everyone by holding out her hand and manipulating the water, shaping it into dolphins. The man opposite her laughed, took a leisurely sip of coffee, and then gave a sharp nod toward her water dolphin, which instantly turned into an ice sculpture.

I burst into an enthusiastic round of applause, causing everyone to swivel round and look in our direction. There was a ripple of whispers that echoed throughout the dome and I quickly stopped clapping.

"Everyone is very excited that you're here," David explained, as Dad put an arm around my shoulders. "They've all been waiting to see the ... light stone... What was it called again?"

"The Light of the World," Dad informed him.

"And they'll have to wait a little longer to see it," Mum said sternly. "We will be keeping it under lock and key until the main conference in a couple of days."

"The Vermore security systems are the best in the world," David assured her. "Mr. Vermore told me to let you know that if you want to put it somewhere other than your room before the conference, then he'd be happy to—"

"That's all right," Mum answered, cutting him off. "It's very secure and he did inform me there's a safe in the room?"

"Oh, aye," David nodded, adjusting his glasses. "The safe in your room is the best Vermore one there is. It's only, Mr. Vermore has a personal vault, and he mentioned you might want to keep it there instead."

Mum and Dad shared a look.

"Please thank Mr. Vermore on my behalf, but we'll hold on to it for now."

Mum and Dad hadn't even told *me* exactly where the Light of the World was. We'd learned from the night at the Natural History Museum that just being near the precious stone made my matching swirled scar glow brightly and made my powers very volatile, but Dad had informed me that they'd managed to have a special small box designed for it that was made of such an incredible metal – a hundred times stronger than the vaults the stone had been kept in at the museum – that I wouldn't be so affected with it being nearby.

And considering my powers hadn't been out of control and my scar hadn't been glowing at all for the entire journey here when they had the stone on them, I'm guessing the specially designed box worked.

"Well," Dad said, clearing his throat and pretending not to notice everyone in the dome staring at us, "shall we continue?"

"I … I don't have time to give you a full tour of the complex," David said apologetically, his shoulders hunched forward. "But if you follow me to your rooms, I can point out some of the main features. That door there" – he pointed at one of the doors set into the dome – "leads off to the superhero training room. It has all the equipment you need."

"Sounds great!" Mum said enthusiastically.

"And that is where the meetings will be held over the next two days," David continued, pointing out the next circular door. "On the opposite side of the dome, that door over there leads to the canteen. And your rooms are this way."

He tripped over his foot again, stumbling forward but managing to stay upright this time. He blushed and scurried on, leading us past another large circular door.

"Poor guy," Mum whispered to me, frowning. "His boss clearly terrifies him."

I nodded in agreement, stepping after Dad and David through the spiral door right at the back of the dome. It led to a long, wide corridor of bedrooms.

"Miss Aurora Beam, this is your room."
David knocked loudly.

"Who is it?" a voice behind the door replied.

"It's only me, David Donnelly. Your new

roommate has arrived."

The door swung open and a boy who looked just older than me stood in the doorway. He examined me with his intense dark eyes before letting out an impatient sigh and standing aside.

"Come in," he said. "And hurry up. I'm hungry and Cherry wouldn't let me go to dinner until you'd arrived."

"I thought it would be nice to all go together."

A tall, very pretty girl wearing headphones round her neck stepped round him and gave me a warm smile. Her long hair was black at the roots and dyed bright blue on the ends.

"Hi, Aurora."

"Hi," I squeaked back, suddenly feeling very shy.

"You three are the only superhero children attending the conference, so we thought it would be nice for you all to stick together.

You girls will take this room, and JJ will take the adjoining suite. Now, if it's all right with you," David said, checking his watch. "I'll take your parents to their room and let you settle in."

"Good idea," Dad nodded. "Aurora, we'll leave you to make some friends!"

ARGH. Why do parents have a knack of always saying the WORST things in front of EVERYONE?!

My cheeks began to burn in embarrassment as the boy attempted to hide a snigger and Cherry gave him a sharp elbow in the ribs.

"We'll see you in the canteen!" Mum said cheerily, waving as she and Dad followed David farther down the corridor.

The others stood aside for me as I wheeled my suitcase into our bedroom.

"That's your bed," the girl told me, pointing to a single bed without any clothes scattered around it.

I thanked her, moving my stuff across to it, and then turned to find them both watching me.

"I'm Cherry Mirella," she said, holding her hand out and shaking mine firmly.

"And I'm Benjamin Jackson Junior. Everyone calls me JJ."

"Nice to meet you," I said quietly. "I'm Aurora Beam."

"We know who you are. You're the reason everyone is here." JJ paused and looked me up and down. "So, what *exactly* is so special about your powers?"

"Don't worry," Cherry said quickly, shooting JJ a look. "He doesn't mean that in a horrible way. You get used to him eventually. We were just talking about our superpowers before you arrived."

I smiled at her gratefully while JJ scowled.

"So," he prompted, folding his arms, "is it true what all those articles say online? That you can create light?"

I nodded.

"And you're connected to the Light of the World," Cherry exclaimed, her eyes wide with fascination. "That's so cool."

"What about you?" I asked, keen to move the focus away from me, but also excited to find out about other kids with superpowers, like me.

"I'm superfast and superstrong," JJ announced proudly. "Super awesome at sports and athletics too."

Cherry rolled her eyes, adding sarcastically,

"And *super* modest."

"The Nigerian soccer team BEGGED me to join them," JJ continued, ignoring her. "But Dad wouldn't let me because I'm only fourteen."

"Wow," I said, before turning to Cherry. "What are your superpowers?"

"I have supersonic hearing." She tapped the headphones round her neck. "I can hear things for miles, hence these specially designed headphones. I can never go anywhere without them. They have all these cool settings on them to help me control what levels I can hear."

"Oh!" I said, before lowering my voice to a whisper. "Does that mean we're hurting your brain right now by speaking so loudly?"

She shook her head.

"I can switch the supersonic hearing on and off through concentration. I only use it when I need to." She grinned mischievously.

"And that's not all she can do," JJ said. "Tell

her about the other thing."

"I sort of have … premonitions," Cherry said, sitting down on her bed.

"Premonitions? As in, you can tell the *future*?" I stared at her in amazement.

"No, not really; it's not as simple as that. I can't tell anything specific. I just get this really strong feeling when something *meaningful* is about to happen. But I have no idea what." She shrugged. "It can be quite inconvenient sometimes."

"I bet."

She smiled at me. "Do you live here in London?"

"No, I'm from Hertfordshire. But we come to London quite often. My dad works in one of the big museums here."

"That's seriously cool," she said, while JJ looked bored. "I'm from Malaysia and this is my first time to London. I thought I'd be able to get in some sightseeing, but" – she gestured to the curved ceiling above her – "it turns out we're stuck underground."

"Who cares about sightseeing? Old buildings and boring galleries." JJ snorted. "We're in an underground *superhero complex*. Why would you want to be anywhere else?"

Cherry rolled her eyes and he turned his attention to me. "So, Aurora, are you game for tomorrow?"

"Game for what?"

"The meetings tomorrow are for adult superheroes only. We're not allowed to take part."

"Oh." I was disappointed. "That's annoying."

"Are you kidding?" JJ looked at me as though I was mad. "It's brilliant. We have the place to ourselves while all the grown-ups have to listen to boring people drone on about some boring stone."

"Hey!" Cherry frowned. "That stone is the most precious stone in the world. And the

Beam family powers are anything but boring. They're the most powerful."

JJ grinned. "Which brings me nicely to my point. Let's see whose powers really *are* the best tomorrow. I vote we go to the training room while our parents are in the meeting and then we can see *exactly* what we can all do."

"You are the most competitive person I have ever met." Cherry sighed, rolling her eyes. "But I suppose that does sound quite fun."

I hesitated, remembering my pathetic attempt to summon my superpowers in Nanny Beam's underground lair. They were hardly going to be impressed by a few sparks. But I didn't want to let them down.

"All right," I said, doing my best to be optimistic. "I'm in."

"Yes!" JJ said, punching the air. "May the best superhero win!"

11

JJ sat down next to me, his eyes bright with excitement.

"I just spoke to Dad," he said, gesturing to a man sitting at another table who looked exactly like JJ, but a bigger and taller version. "He confirmed that the next meeting starts in half an hour, so the training room will be completely free."

"Did he say anything about this morning's meeting?" I asked, waving at Mum and Dad who had just walked into the canteen to get their lunch and sit with JJ's and Cherry's parents.

"Not really. Apparently it was just your parents giving them all the information about the Light of the World."

"That makes sense." Cherry nodded. "You need to know all the information about something before you can make an informed decision as to what to do about it."

I smiled. "You sound just like my friend Kizzy."

I was really missing my best friend. It felt like so long that I had been away from the Bright Sparks and there was no mobile signal underground so I couldn't message them. I even missed Suzie going on and on about her new routines and almost hitting me in the head when she spontaneously decided to do a cartwheel.

"It must be weird that your friends know about your superpowers," Cherry commented, taking a sip of her water. "I saw that they helped you stop that Blackout Burglar from getting away with the precious stones."

"They were key to the operation," I said proudly. "I couldn't have done it without them. And Alfred, my aunt's pet ostrich."

JJ looked confused. "Your aunt has a pet ostrich?"

"Yes. He's really into fashion. And breaking things."

"I wish I could tell my friends about my powers. It's quite difficult keeping it all under wraps," Cherry said.

"Same," JJ agreed, pushing his broccoli to the other side of his plate. "I always have to run much slower in races and sometimes in stuff like soccer I forget and kick the ball right into the goal from the other end of the pitch. Mum and Dad get really mad at me. You're so lucky."

"I guess so. It was hard at first though, so I know what you mean. My friends only found out about my powers by accident," I said, absentmindedly tracing the swirled scar on my palm with my finger.

"Does your dad have any superpowers?" JJ asked, as we overheard Dad launch into a conversation with Cherry's parents, Sky and Saheed, about the "fascinating structure of crystalline material."

"No, he's a professor of mineralogy at the Natural History Museum. Are *your* parents both superheroes?"

"Yeah, they met on the job," JJ explained. "My dad has super strength, he's practically invincible. Mum, well, she—"

But he didn't need to finish his sentence because, at that moment, JJ's mum appeared through *the wall* of the canteen, kissing his dad on the cheek and apologizing for being late to lunch.

The three of us burst out laughing.

"Yeah, no explanation needed," JJ said. "I was hoping I might develop the ability to walk through walls since I got Dad's superstrength gene, but every time I've tried, I've just run straight into them and knocked myself out."

"Now, that sounds extremely entertaining," Cherry said. "Maybe you should keep practicing."

"What about your parents, Cherry?" I asked, eagerly. "Are they superheroes, too?"

"Just my mum. She has the power of invisibility, a bit like Crystal."

"Whooooa." JJ nodded, impressed. "That is awesome."

Cherry smiled. "Not when she decides to play pranks on you. Trust me, I've had a hundred frights when she just appears out of nowhere."

I watched as Mr. Vermore sauntered into the bustling canteen and gave a sharp nod to his assistant, David, who had sidled up next to him.

David acknowledged Mr. Vermore's gesture by calling for everyone to quiet down, but nobody was listening. He tried again, Mr. Vermore narrowing his eyes at him in frustration, but David's voice was drowned out by the sound of cutlery clattering and friendly chatter.

Eventually, Mr. Vermore gave up on his assistant's attempts and announced in a loud booming voice, "Good afternoon, superheroes!"

The canteen immediately settled to a hush.

"I hope you are all enjoying your lunch, courtesy of Vermore Enterprises," he said smugly. "Now, please do begin to make your way to the main conference room for the second meeting of the day. And, as I may have mentioned before, if any of you would like to discuss any of my very exciting future business opportunities, my door is always open before and after the meetings. Although, I mean that metaphorically, of course," he added quickly. "Please do knock and don't barge in. Anyway, enjoy your lunch and remember, *Vermore, for people who want more!*"

He turned on his heel and marched out of the canteen. JJ shook his head as the chatter began again.

"They shouldn't allow non-superheroes at a Superhero Conference. Especially not cheesy businessmen."

"They had to let Mr. Vermore be a part of it," Cherry pointed out. "He's the one who provided all the technology and security systems. Not to mention he renovated this place."

"Mr. Vermore built all this?"

"Well, according to my mum, whenever a Superhero Conference has taken place in London, it's always been under the Houses of Parliament, but it never used to be as cool as this dome thing," Cherry explained. "He paid for it to be spruced up a few years ago when he was brought on as the sponsor."

"How did he know about the Superhero Conference in the first place if he's not a superhero?" JJ frowned.

Cherry shrugged. "He must have a contact," she said. "Anyway, who cares? Are we ready to go to the training room?"

"I was born ready!" JJ said, suddenly straightening up and puffing his chest out. "Let's go."

When JJ pressed the button and ushered us

through the door to the training room – "I love these doors; it's like being on a spaceship" – I thought we'd taken a wrong turn because right in the center was a big yellow school bus.

"I think we've got the wrong room," I said, frowning. "Maybe it's the next one along."

"Nah, this is the training room. Brilliant, isn't it?" JJ said gleefully. "All the walls are padded and can withstand anything you throw at them: fire, ice blasts, cars, the lot. Over there" – he nodded toward a door at the other end of the room – "is the storeroom. It's got whatever equipment a superhero might need to train to stop bad guys."

"But why is there a big school bus in the middle of the training room?" Cherry asked, looking as baffled as I was.

JJ tutted dramatically. "So naive!"

He rolled up his sleeves, said, "Watch this," and then went to stand next to the front of the bus.

"This is why there is a big school bus in the middle of the training room," he announced, before crouching down, facing the bus.

"No … way…" Cherry whispered, as we both watched in anticipation.

JJ slowly but surely began to lift the bus, raising it high above his head. Cherry and I burst into applause and cheers as he held it there for a few seconds before carefully bringing it down again.

Then, as soon as the tires hit the floor again, and without a moment's hesitation, he jumped so high into the air that he landed on the hood of the bus, causing me and Cherry to gasp in chorus. Then he jumped effortlessly up to the roof of the bus and ran so fast the whole way down it that he was almost a blur. He somersaulted off the back, landing perfectly and turning to bow for his audience. He walked back to give us both high fives and then sat down on the floor to catch his breath.

"That was amazing!" I exclaimed, as Cherry nodded in agreement.

"I'm hoping to get stronger as I grow up," JJ said, wiping his forehead with his sleeve. "That's what happened to my dad, anyway. So," he nodded toward Cherry, "your turn."

She grinned, placed her headphones over her ears, fiddling with some settings on their side, and then closed her eyes in concentration.

"There is a very fiery parliament debate happening right now, directly above us," she said, without opening her eyes. "Someone in the debate isn't actually listening; he's playing a game on his phone. Even with the sound off, I can tell he's playing a game because his tapping on the keypad of his phone isn't consistent with texting."

"Wow," I breathed.

"And over here" – she pointed her finger at a different part of the ceiling – "someone is stuffing a lot of chips into their mouth at once. They're eating them weirdly fast. Hang on." She paused before a smile spread across her face. "Now someone else has come into the room and is asking that person if they've seen a bag of chips lying around. The person who just ate them is saying she hasn't. Actually, I recognize that voice! It's the prime minister!"

I giggled.

"How do we know you're not making this all up?" JJ asked suspiciously, getting to his feet and folding his arms.

Cherry sighed, still keeping her eyes closed. "OK, JJ, how about this? I can hear that your digestive system is currently digesting seven ... no, eight chocolate cookies."

JJ's eyes widened. "H ... how did you—"

"And now, because you're embarrassed, I can hear your body releasing adrenaline which is causing your blood vessels to dilate. Your cheeks feel hot, right?"

"Yeah," he gulped.

"And I can hear that David Donnelly has just left Mr. Vermore's office and is currently heading toward this room. His pace is slowing which means he's likely to be coming to check on us and will be coming through the door riiiiiiiight ... now."

The door opened and David scuttled in, giving us a wave. "Everything all right in here? You kids enjoying the training room?"

"Very much," I said, beaming at Cherry.

"David, you might want to hurry back to your bedroom," Cherry instructed. "I can hear something burning in there."

"My scented candles!" he gasped. "I forgot to check that they were out!"

As he darted away, JJ shook his head and held up his hands. "OK, I'll admit that was pretty awesome. Can you hear what's going on in the superhero meeting right now?"

Cherry shook her head and lowered her headphones back around her neck.

"They've superhero proofed that main meeting room. Mr. Vermore's technology somehow blocks me from hearing anything that goes on in there. It's just muffled noise."

"Any premonitions you have that you can

tell us about?"

"I can't switch those on and off," Cherry said and shrugged. "I have no control over when I'm going to get them."

JJ nodded before he turned to look at me. "Your turn!"

"All right," I said nervously. "But you should know I haven't practiced in a while and the last time I tried, things went a bit … wrong."

JJ laughed. "I saw that online; you took out some famous presenters or something. TV comedy gold."

"Take your time, Aurora," Cherry encouraged. "It's only us."

I nodded and tried to focus, doing my best to ignore my nerves and push away the memories of my powers being completely out of control at the TV studio. I desperately tried to feel that hot, tingling feeling of the powers rushing through my veins, dazzling light beams bursting from my palms.

But all I felt was my hands getting clammier as the others waited for something to happen. My heart sank.

"Come on," I whispered to myself, ignoring Cherry and JJ sharing a look. *"Come on."*

My hands got a bit warmer and some white sparks burst from my fingertips along with a gentle glow, but it was nothing like the light

beams I'd created at the Natural History Museum when foiling

Mr. Mercury's plot to steal the precious stones.

"I'm sorry," I said, dropping my hands to my side and clenching my fists. "I just... I can't do it anymore. I'm hopeless."

"That was still really great," Cherry said, smiling at me. "Maybe you've just lost your confidence a bit. You want to try again?"

I shook my head, my cheeks growing hot with embarrassment.

They stood awkwardly for a moment and then Cherry gave JJ a nudge. "Hey, bet you can't lift the whole bus with one hand."

"Oh yeah?" He raised his eyebrows and then raced toward the bus. "You just watch."

I waited until he was out of earshot and then caught her eye.

"Thanks," I said, grateful to her for changing the subject.

For the rest of the day, Cherry and JJ talked excitedly about each other's powers and how cool they were, tactfully avoiding any mention of mine. That evening as I got into my pajamas, I pushed my Lightning Girl sneakers under the bed. I didn't deserve them. I didn't feel like Lightning Girl at all these days. Maybe that time at the Natural History Museum was a fluke. I wasn't the superhero that everyone thought I was.

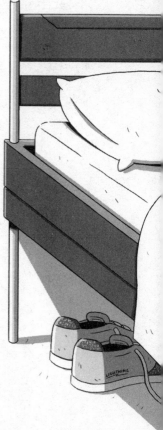

"Aurora," Cherry whispered into the darkness once the lights were off. "Are you awake?"

"Yes," I replied over the sound of JJ snoring next door. I'd been lying awake thinking about the next day's events, and when the decision would be made about the Light of the World.

"I ... I just had a premonition."

I sat bolt upright in bed. "Cool!"

"No, Aurora. It's not cool. I don't know what on earth it is," she said, her voice shaking. "But I think something bad is going to happen."

12

The next day, Cherry, JJ and I stood outside my parents' bedroom knocking loudly.

"Good morning," Mum said, stunned to open the door and see us all crowded in her doorway. "Is everything all right?"

"We're not sure. Can we come in?"

Mum nodded and stepped aside to let us into the room where Dad was sitting on the bed tying his shoelaces.

"Hello." He smiled warmly. "Are you all coming down to breakfast with us?"

"We need to talk to you about something important," I said firmly. "JJ, shut the door behind you."

He did as I instructed.

Mum folded her arms. "What's going on?"

I nodded to Cherry, giving her the go-ahead, and she nervously stepped forward.

"Last night I had a premonition. It's one of my powers," she explained. "And it wasn't good."

"What do you mean?"

"It's hard to explain, but I just know something bad is going to happen. I have no idea what but..."

She trailed off and I took over.

"But, considering that today is the day the final decision will be made on what to do with the Light of the World, it seems a bit weird."

"I can't be sure," Cherry said, letting out a long sigh. "But it seems odd that I would get a bad premonition the night before such a huge moment, don't you think?"

"Mum," I began firmly, "I think you should cancel the conference today. We should take the Light of the World home with us."

"What?" Mum shook her head in disbelief. "Aurora, I can't just *cancel* the conference! We have gathered everyone here for this reason; people have traveled a long way, literally from all over the Earth. We've had long, tiring meetings yesterday just to get to this point."

"But the Light of the World might be in danger!"

"Maybe my premonition has nothing to do with the precious stone," Cherry jumped in, looking worried. "It could be nothing. I'm probably just making a fuss."

"I don't think we should take the risk," I declared.

"But even if the premonition *is* about the

Light of the World, would it really be safer at home with you?" JJ pointed out. "The security systems here are the best in the world and there's no chance that someone can get past all the superheroes."

"That's true," Dad said, watching me carefully. "Surely if it is in danger, the safest place would be here, where it is protected."

Mum pointed at the high-tech safe in the corner of the room. "That safe is unbreakable, even to superpowers. I'm the only person who knows how to access it and even if anyone were

to crack that – which they can't – the Light of the World is still in the box that your dad and I had specially designed for it.

Aurora, the box is so strong that the stone has no effect on your powers when you're nearby. Remember the Natural History Museum? You only had to be in the same building as that stone for your powers to be sent out of control."

"Yes, but—"

"Trust me, it's safe with us."

There was a light rapping of knuckles on the door.

"Hello? May I come in?"

Mum stepped past JJ, opening the door to Mr. Vermore and David Donnelly, who stood anxiously behind his boss.

"Everything all right in here?" Mr. Vermore asked, his small sharp eyes darting from one of us to another.

"Yes, of course," Mum said cheerily. "We were just about to make our way to breakfast."

Mr. Vermore checked his watch and raised

his eyebrows at her.

"Well, you had better get going, it will be cleared soon. I heard raised voices in here." He paused, watching Cherry as she stared down at her shoes. "What's going on?"

"Nothing," Dad insisted. "Just a healthy debate."

"I thought I heard something about the Light of the World being in danger," he pressed. "If that's so, I think I should know about it."

"It's my fault," Cherry squeaked, unable to look anyone in the eye. "It was a silly premonition that I had."

"A premonition?" Mr. Vermore towered over her. "What premonition?"

"Cherry had a bad premonition about today," JJ explained. "And we just thought we should let Mr. and Mrs. Beam know, in case it was something to do with the Light of the World."

"You don't think it's safe here?" He sniffed, looking insulted.

"I think we should take it home and cancel the conference," I said, crossing my arms.

He turned slowly to face me. "You think *what?*"

"Mr. Vermore, if there's any chance that the Light of the World is in danger and Cherry's premonition is right, then I don't think we should risk it."

"Miss Beam," he said, his expression changing from concern to amusement, "I can assure you that the Vermore safe over there is unbreakable. Only your mother has access. And there are other security measures in place on top of that. Now, are you *sure* this isn't about something else?"

"What do you mean?"

He smiled down at me sympathetically. "I can imagine that it must have been very nice to have had the Light of the World in your possession all this time. After all, it is the source of the Beam family superpowers and therefore, it would be very natural to feel that it belongs to you. And today's outcome may well sway in your favor, but either way, you must understand that this is ultimately the most responsible method of choosing the fate of something so powerful—"

"I am NOT trying to keep the stone for

myself," I protested, my cheeks growing hot with anger. "Cherry had a premonition and I—"

"I'm sure it was to do with something else," Cherry interjected, looking mortified. "Please, let's just leave it and go to breakfast. It may have been about something completely different."

"You see?" Mr. Vermore said, clapping his hands together triumphantly. "Canceling the conference would be an extreme overreaction. Now, if you don't hurry along to breakfast, you'll miss it entirely and it wouldn't do to go through such an important day on an empty stomach, would it?"

Mum placed an arm around my shoulders as Mr. Vermore held open the door for us. JJ and Cherry traipsed out behind him into the corridor.

"Mum, Dad," I said, looking at them

pleadingly. "You don't believe I want the precious stone for myself, do you?"

"Of course not!" Dad said firmly. "We understand that you're worried."

Mum nodded in agreement. "And we'll keep everything you've said in mind. If we have any inkling that something isn't right, we'll take the Light of the World and get out of here in a flash."

I sighed, defeated. "All right. I'll see you down at breakfast. I want to check something. You go ahead."

They shared a worried glance but didn't say anything, leaving me alone in the bedroom. I crouched down at the safe and examined it closely. I guess it seemed pretty sturdy. There were hundreds of buttons all around the edge, so it was obviously not your average safe.

I stood up and shook my head, trying to get rid of the niggling feeling Cherry had lodged in my brain. I left the room and made my way toward the canteen. As I walked down the corridor, I heard a sharp voice and stopped when I realized it belonged to Mr. Vermore. He was just around the corner, speaking to someone.

I stopped, pressing myself up against the wall, and waited, listening closely.

"Are you saying that I'm *wrong*?" Mr. Vermore was growling.

"N ... no, of course not," the shaky voice of David Donnelly replied. "But... I just... If Cherry's premonition is right, surely we need to make sure the precious stone is safely—"

"Mr. Donnelly, you seem to have forgotten your place!" Mr. Vermore snapped. "I've worked too hard for this moment. You... Well, let's just say that you have no idea of the work that has gone in to setting this all up exactly how I planned. And no one is going to stop this conference going ahead. Especially not a bunch of *teenagers*. Is that understood?"

I heard a vague whimper and then the sound of Mr. Vermore's designer shoes thudding away down the corridor, followed closely by David Donnelly's squeaking soles, scampering to keep up with him.

I had an overwhelming urge to speak to the Bright Sparks and let them reassure me that I wasn't overreacting about all this. Kizzy was so smart and sensible, she would be able to tell me if I was being silly or not. But according to David Donnelly, who I'd asked on the first day, the only place to get a mobile signal down here was Mr. Vermore's office.

And I wasn't going to go ask him if I could make a call to my friends.

Because, after overhearing that conversation, I didn't trust Mr. Vermore one bit.

An hour later, I took my place next to Cherry and JJ in the conference theater, watching as Mum and Dad chatted in the middle of the stage to Mr. Vermore and David. Mum caught my eye in the audience and smiled encouragingly. On the front of the stage was a podium on which there was a simple silver box. You would never believe that it contained the most precious stone in the world.

"You see?" JJ said, giving me a nudge with his elbow. "It's right there."

"Yeah. I guess I overreacted."

"It's understandable that you did," Cherry said kindly. "That precious stone means a lot more to you than anyone else in the room. I shouldn't have told you about my premonition and caused such a fuss about nothing."

Mr. Vermore cleared his throat and marched to center stage, basking in the spotlights. A hush descended around the room.

"Good morning, superheroes! Today is the day that you shall come to an informed decision on where the Light of the World would be safest. Your previous meetings have concluded with two sensible options for the future of this most precious of stones. Today shall be the deciding vote."

He took a dramatically deep breath.

"Yes," he continued, acting as though he

was a big movie star shooting an epic battle-cry scene. "Should the stone be returned to where the Beam family believes it belongs, beneath the aurora borealis, or northern lights, if you will?" He paused, enjoying the flush of whispers. "Or, should the precious stone be kept in the safest of safe places, a place that can be monitored and checked" – he took another deep breath, before bellowing – "a Vermore high-security, unbreakable vault!"

There was another ripple of murmurs across the audience.

"It is time to put it to a vote. The decision is in your hands. May you choose the safest, most secure, tried and tested option for this stone so precious in our hearts. The Light of the World. Over to you, Mrs. Beam," he said, bowing as he exited the stage to a weak round of applause and gesturing angrily for David to follow him.

Mum stepped forward to stand next to the podium, resting her hand protectively on the box.

"Thank you for your patience. After all the hard work, I think it's about time you were allowed to see the Light of the World as we decide together on its fate," she said to the crowd.

I could feel the tension soar as everyone craned forward in excitement and anticipation.

After a few moments of pressing several buttons on the side of the box, as well as fishing out what looked like a very weirdly shaped key from her pocket to unlock it, Mum opened the lid. There was a collective gasp from the room and Mum stumbled backward in horror.

"*No,*" she whispered.

The box was empty.

13

The conference room erupted into chaos and panic.

Mum was frozen to the spot as Dad hurried over to be at her side. Cherry had clasped her hand over her mouth in shock and all the color had drained from JJ's face.

Mr. Vermore came thundering back up the steps to the stage, roaring, "IMPOSSIBLE! IT CAN'T BE! IT'S IMPOSSIBLE!"

"How could this happen?" someone shouted from behind me in the audience. "How could you *let* this happen?"

Mum was shaking her head in disbelief. "It was there," she was saying over and over as Dad put a comforting arm around her. "I checked this morning! It was right *there*!"

"Someone must have taken it!" a superhero across the room yelled at the top of his lungs.

"That's not possible!" Mr. Vermore insisted, looking as though he was about to explode. "My security systems are—"

"Supposedly the best in the world? Clearly not!" JJ's dad cried out, folding his arms stubbornly, gaining murmurs of agreement from the crowd.

"Now, you all look here," Mr. Vermore

snarled. "The locked safe that stone was in, is *unbreakable*. It could only... Well, I suppose it could only..."

"It could only WHAT?" Cherry's mum asked as Mr. Vermore wrung his hands anxiously.

"It could only have been a superhero!" he roared. "That's the only explanation! Someone with extreme powers! And even then, it would be near impossible! I'm telling you, the only explanation is that someone in HERE is the thief!"

"Why would anyone in here take the precious stone?" Crystal said, shaking her head. "We're all here to keep it safe!"

"What about the Beams?" a voice shouted from the back. "Maybe they wanted to keep it for themselves!"

Mum shot such a glare at him from the stage that he shrank back into his seat. But the damage had been done.

"Of course," Mr. Vermore gasped, his eyes flashing at me. "Aurora … you didn't…"

Everyone swiveled to stare in my direction.

"This is nothing to do with Aurora!" Mum growled, as a feeling of panic bubbled through me.

"I would never take the Light of the World!" I said, stung by all their accusing eyes.

"Not for yourself, maybe," Mr. Vermore said, watching me carefully. "Maybe you just took it to protect it. Is that right? You said this morning that you wanted to take it home…"

"I only said that because I thought it was in danger. And I was right, wasn't I?"

His eyes met mine and we glared at each other accusingly.

It had to be him. I *knew* it was him.

No one was going to believe me, but everything pointed to Darek Vermore. The way he wanted the conference to go exactly as planned; how he knew everyone's movements and everything about the safe it had been in; and hadn't I overheard him pretty much admitting it to David earlier? *"I've worked too hard for this moment,"* he'd said. *"You have no idea of the work that has gone in to setting this all up exactly how I planned."*

And here I was, the perfect scapegoat.

"It all sounds like a bizarre coincidence to me," someone called out before I could say anything else. "Aurora tried to make an excuse and when that didn't work, she stole it!"

"Why would I do that?" I asked, fizzing with anger. "No, you have to listen to me; I think I know—"

"Isn't she the niece of Lucinda Beam?" another superhero pointed out as others nodded along with her. "Lucinda is renowned for being light-fingered when it comes to precious jewelry. It runs in the family! Aurora may have learned a few tips!"

"There is no chance that Aurora had anything to do with this!" Mum cried out, clutching the empty box. "She has only ever wanted to protect the Light of the World!"

"Please, listen!" I cried, but no one heard.

"But the precious stone has *her* scar on it!" a man sitting in the front row said, turning to narrow his eyes at me. "Maybe she felt she had the right to it!"

"Maybe she and Lucinda Beam are in it together!"

"I say, we search her room!"

"I say, we make sure that she can't escape the conference until we have discovered it!"

The room burst into noise as everyone spoke over everyone else, trying to make their opinion heard. Mum and Dad tried to get everyone to calm down so that they could protest my innocence, but nobody was listening to them.

I turned to JJ and Cherry. "You guys don't believe any of this, do you?"

"No, I don't think so," JJ said nervously, biting his lip. "Although, we have only known you a day or so... Maybe you've been fooling us. Maybe you want it for your powers to work..."

"*What*?" I stared at them in shock. "I would never... Please, you have to believe me."

"Aurora," Cherry said gently, "we'd completely understand if you'd taken it just to make sure it was safe. We know you wouldn't want it for yourself" – she shot a pointed look at JJ, who blushed – "but maybe you took it because you thought it might be in danger at the conference? Is that why you were hanging back on your own in your parents' room before breakfast? You can tell us; we'd understand."

I shook my head, swallowing the lump building up in my throat and fighting back tears.

"I didn't take the Light of the World. And if you knew me like my friends the Bright Sparks do, you would know that I would never do that."

David Donnelly had by now run up to the stage with a pair of cymbals and, prompted by a sharp nod from Mr. Vermore, he clashed them loudly together, making everyone jump and fall to a sudden silence.

"Thank you, David. I thought those might come in handy," Mr. Vermore said, before taking a deep breath. "Superheroes, I have just instructed David to put the conference into lockdown. The building is completely secured. No one can get in or out. We will search the building until the Light of the World is found, and commence crisis talks."

"What about Aurora?" someone called out.

"*What about her*?" Mum seethed.

"Perhaps for peace of mind, Aurora should go to her room," Mr. Vermore said carefully. "Just until we find the stone. If she's innocent, then she has nothing to worry about and all this will be cleared up."

"I don't think that's necessary," Crystal said, glaring at him and receiving a grateful look from Mum and Dad. "She doesn't look like a mastermind thief to me."

"I think Mr. Vermore has a good point!

Aurora Beam is the main suspect," another superhero insisted from the back of the room. "We should put it to a vote!"

"Good idea," a woman with bright-green spiky hair nodded. "She should be sent to her room until we find out where she's stowed the precious stone."

"That way, we'll know for sure and keep Aurora safe from further rumors, too," Mr. Vermore said to my mum who was looking at him so angrily that her eyes had narrowed to slits. "I'm sorry. If there was another way…"

"I didn't take the Light of the World!" I wailed, springing to my feet and clenching my fists. "Mr. Vermore—"

"Let's put it to a vote!" the man at the back declared, speaking over me and prompting a murmur of agreement from the audience. "All those in favor of shutting Aurora Beam safely in her room until the crisis is over, stand up."

Slowly, people began to rise to their feet. It was an overwhelming majority. At least Cherry and JJ stayed firmly sitting in their seats.

"This is ridiculous!" Dad yelled, exasperated. "How can any of you possibly think this has anything to do with Aurora! She's just about to turn twelve years old!"

"The heroes have spoken!" the spiky-haired lady announced. "Mr. Vermore, escort Aurora to her room at once and please make sure that she is locked in there for the time being. We can do a full search of her room."

"Sorry, Beams." Mr. Vermore sighed. "My hands are tied."

He gestured to David to do as she said. Under everyone's scrutinizing watch, David walked through the audience, and gently ushered me down the row and toward the door.

"I haven't taken the stone!" I protested. "Ask Mr. Vermore!"

"Aurora, everything will be all right," Dad called out as Mum stood next to him, completely gobsmacked. "We'll sort it, don't you worry."

David led me back through the silent, empty dome to my bedroom and hesitated at the door as I slumped on my bed, a tear rolling down my cheek.

How had this happened?!

"Don't worry," he said sympathetically, looking pained at his task. "This will all be over soon, I'm sure. They'll hold a big crisis meeting and then we'll be able to work out what's happened to it."

"I didn't take it," I whispered, burying my head in my hands.

There was a pause before David said quietly, "I believe you."

And then he shut the door, turned the key in the lock, and the sound of his footsteps disappeared down the corridor.

Someone rapped their knuckles gently on the bedroom door.

"Aurora? Aurora, are you there?"

I slid off my bed and pressed my ear against the door. "Cherry?"

"Hey," she said, "it's me and JJ. Are you all right?"

"Yes," I lied.

For the past half an hour I'd been knocking on all the walls of the room, trying to work out if there was a secret hidden escape route.

I'd even tried picking the lock with some hair clips, but it turned out that picking locks is a LOT harder in real life than they make it look in movies.

"We wanted to tell you that we believe that you didn't take the precious stone," Cherry continued, as I sat on the floor with my back against the door listening to them. "We're so sorry that we doubted you."

"Yeah," JJ jumped in. "There's no way you would have had time to work out how to break into the safe and take the stone in those few minutes you held back before breakfast."

I then heard JJ hiss, "Ouch!" and guessed that he'd received an elbow in the ribs from Cherry.

"Obviously, that's *not* the reason we believe you though," she corrected pointedly, as JJ grumbled about bruising easily. "We believe you because you're our friend."

"Thanks," I said through the door. "That means a lot. But I'm still stuck in here and nobody else believes me. And more importantly, the Light of the World is missing. Any updates?"

"All the grown-ups are having a crisis talk in the conference room, so I can't hear anything that's going on," Cherry explained. "But I was able to listen in on Mr. Vermore talking to David and your parents as they walked along a corridor a few minutes ago. Apparently, it's all over the press and the Internet."

"*What?*"

"Yeah, it's bad," JJ said. "It's all over social media. They know everything now about the secret Superhero Conference *and* about the Light of the World going missing. Cherry could hear Mr. Vermore complaining about how he was going to have to hold a press conference to discuss how the most precious stone on the planet got stolen out from under the best security measures in the world. He's furious."

"How could anyone possibly know?" I asked, shaking my head. "How would anyone be able to leak the news to social media? There's no signal anywhere … except in Mr. Vermore's office!"

"Someone in here is up to something," Cherry said firmly. "Aurora, someone is trying to frame you."

"All the news reports online are stating that you're the main suspect," JJ added.

"And I think I know who it is," I said firmly. "Mr. Vermore is behind all this."

There was a hesitation before Cherry spoke. "But, Aurora, why would he make himself look bad? His safe is supposed to be unbreakable. He's furious about the leaks to the press; he said his company's name is being dragged through the dirt."

"I have a gut feeling about him," I argued.

"You're going to need more than a gut feeling to persuade everyone," JJ pointed out. "He's a bit slimy and annoying, yeah, but don't you think if he wanted the stone, he'd have done it in a more ... I don't know ... publicity-friendly way?"

"He genuinely looked upset that the stone was missing," Cherry said.

"He made sure that I got the blame AND he went ballistic just at the idea of canceling the conference, probably because he had planned out exactly the right moment to steal the stone. And the only place you can get a signal to leak the stories is his office," I said stubbornly. "Thanks to him, everyone in the world now thinks that I'm a thief!"

"Not everyone," JJ said quickly. "We don't. We're going to help find the truth!"

I smiled as I pictured him on the other

side of the door in a proud superhero stance as he said that. I could practically hear Cherry giving him a dramatic eye roll.

"How can I help find the truth when I'm locked in here?"

"Aha!" JJ said. "We were getting to that. Move away from the door, Aurora. We're coming in!"

"What?"

"Hang on," Cherry hissed grumpily at him, "we need to check that the coast is clear."

"The coast *is* clear."

"I need to double-check that no one is coming down the corridor," Cherry argued.

"Well, hurry up then!" JJ huffed. "Get your headphones on and listen!"

"Stop bossing me about. I'm older than you!"

"Guys?" I said, clearing my throat. "Any chance you can tell me what's going on?"

"Everybody quiet for a moment," Cherry

said, and JJ and I fell into silence.

After a minute or so, she spoke.

"OK, no one is coming for a bit. Now's a good time to give it a try."

"Good. Aurora, stand back from the door!" JJ instructed.

I leapt to my feet and hurried over to my bed, jumping up onto it with my back against the wall, holding my breath in anticipation.

"Here we go!" I heard JJ yell.

There was a sudden patter of very fast footsteps and then a loud *CLUNK!*

After a moment's silence, Cherry exploded into shrieks of laughter and I could hear JJ groaning in pain.

"That ... was ... brilliant!" Cherry wheezed in between infectious giggles. "Aurora ... if ... you ... could ... have ... seen..."

"What happened?" I asked, running back to the door and pressing myself up against it.

"Stop laughing! Stop laughing!" JJ yelled. "It's NOT FUNNY!"

"Cherry, what happened?"

"He just ran straight into the door!" Cherry said, bursting into a fresh round of laughter. "You should have seen his face! Oh man, I wish I'd filmed it."

"Why did you run into the door, JJ?" I asked in confusion.

"He was trying to break it down with his super strength," Cherry chuckled. "I'm crying with laughter! I'm *crying*!"

"Mr. Vermore must have made these doors very strong," I heard JJ huff. "How was I supposed to know?"

"It was brave of you to try," I said, stifling a laugh just at the thought of JJ running at the door full force. "Thanks anyway."

"Yeah, well, what are we going to do now?" JJ mumbled. "That was our only plan for getting you out."

"We'll have to think of something else," Cherry said, still giggling.

Suddenly, I heard another voice floating down the corridor in the distance.

"That won't be necessary."

Cherry stopped laughing and I could make out two pairs of footsteps, one heavier than the other, coming toward them.

"Who is it?" I whispered.

"Who ... who are you?" Cherry asked.

There was no response, just scuffles of noise as Cherry and JJ were seemingly ushered away from the door.

"Cherry? JJ?" I squeaked. "Who is it? What's going on?"

But there was no answer. I looked down at the lock as I heard the satisfying clicking of it being opened. I stepped back fearfully, with no idea about what was happening.

Suddenly, the door swung open and standing triumphantly in the doorway with a hair pin in his mouth was...

"ALFRED!" I cried.

I was so happy to see him that, for a moment, I forgot that he was the grumpiest ostrich in the world and I ran full pelt at him to give him a hug. His eyes widened in horror at the sight of me hurtling toward him and he immediately lifted one of his legs up in front of him, halting me in my tracks and holding me at bay with his scaly bird foot.

"Well," I sighed, moving back from him and holding up my hands. "It's good to see you anyway."

He dropped his long leg and then ruffled his feathers irritably, stalking past me into the bedroom to inspect the beds and peck at the pillows. Today, he was wearing a white panama hat and a pink-and-white striped jacket draped over his shoulders.

"Alfred has always been adept at picking locks," Aunt Lucinda said, stepping into the room behind him and fondly watching him rip my pillow apart.

She held out her arms and ushered me in for a brief hug.

"Careful, darling," she said, patting me on the head. "You'll crease my jacket — a prince gave this particular one to me, so it's really one of a kind."

"What are you *doing* here?" I asked.

JJ and Cherry had wandered in behind Aunt Lucinda and were glancing back and forth between Alfred and her in complete amazement.

"Alfred and I were having a marvelous time lunching on the Southbank when we heard the news about the Superhero Conference. So much for a big secret. The whole world knows about it now," she explained with a long sigh. "Your name is everywhere, Aurora, and I'm afraid it's not good."

"They think I stole the Light of the World."

She grimaced. "Yes, that is what everyone is saying," she said. "My name has been dragged into the mix as well. A lot of comments about us being in it together, which frankly I find particularly vexing." She shook her head. "If I was going to steal the Light of the World, I wouldn't do nearly such a sloppy job of it and I certainly wouldn't have waited until now."

"Are you a superhero, too?" JJ asked, cutting in.

Aunt Lucinda raised her eyebrows at him and tutted.

"Hardly, darling. Do you think I could maintain this fabulous hairstyle being a hero? But if you're asking if I have superpowers, the answer is yes. Like all the Beam women. I just chose to use mine in a much more efficient manner than saving the world."

"How did you get into the conference so late?" I said, trying to ignore Alfred as he wandered through the door to JJ's room and started examining the pile of clothes on his bed.

"Oh, very simple," Aunt Lucinda said with a wave of her hand. "Before the conference, Crystal and I had a long conversation about how to get into it, should I change my mind and decide to turn up a day or so late. She gave me full instructions about the lamppost and made sure the entrance didn't lock after the last superhero had arrived. Crystal and I go way back," she added, smiling. "For her last birthday, I bought her a poodle, Fluffles. He really is very sweet."

"Hey! That's mine!" JJ said suddenly, narrowing his eyes at Alfred.

JJ marched over as Alfred picked up one of JJ's favorite T-shirts with his beak. JJ grabbed hold of one end and attempted to pry it away, but the ostrich held fast against his super strength.

"I wouldn't bother," Aunt Lucinda said breezily. "If he wants it, he has to have it. That's just how it is with ostriches. So, what is the lowdown? I assume Aurora has been locked up in here since the accusations began to abound."

Cherry nodded. "The other superheroes are

all in the main conference room holding a crisis talk about what to do."

Aunt Lucinda looked troubled. "*All* of them?"

"Yes," Cherry replied, glancing at me.

"That's a big mistake." Aunt Lucinda sighed, shaking her head in disappointment.

"What do you mean?"

"Well, if it was *me* who had stolen the Light of the World, right about now I'd be hoping to escape with it. And how better to escape than to make sure *all* the superheroes are locked up in one room, unable to stop me from leaving?"

"But they're not locked up in there," Cherry assured her. "They're just holding a meet—"

Suddenly, a loud alarm bell began ringing through the building and a computerized voice echoed through the speakers.

"Conference room lockdown activated. Conference room lockdown activated."

"Right on cue," Aunt Lucinda said. "Honestly, haven't any of these superheroes stolen anything before? They've been very naive about all this."

"What's happening?" JJ said, giving up on retrieving his T-shirt. Alfred promptly ripped off and ate one of the sleeves.

"What's happening is that all the superheroes have been locked in a superhero-proof conference room," Aunt Lucinda explained. "Someone very clever is about to escape with the Light of the World."

I looked at Cherry's and JJ's panicked expressions and took a deep breath.

"And we're the only ones who can stop them."

15

"We have to get out of here," I said, throwing open my suitcase. "Whoever has stolen the Light of the World will be escaping as we speak. Is the way we came in the only way out?"

Cherry nodded. "Yes, we get the Superhero Express back up to the Houses of Parliament."

"Aunt Lucinda, you and Alfred find the main control room for the security here and try to work out a way of deactivating this lockdown," I instructed.

"We'll see what we can do," she said, heading for the door. "Come along, Alfred!"

The ostrich stalked out of the room behind her, now wearing JJ's sunglasses.

"Will I ever get those back?" JJ sighed, watching Alfred's bottom feathers disappear down the corridor.

"No chance," I replied truthfully, before leading them out of the room. "Let's go!"

"I'll go ahead and get the pod ready," JJ said, suddenly speeding up into a blur and racing through the door leading to the Superhero Express platform.

He was standing beside a waiting pod as Cherry and I ran toward him, before we all strapped ourselves in and braced for the roller-coaster journey back up to the pavement.

"Cherry," I said, as the doors of the pod began to close. "Can you hear anything strange at all?"

She quickly lifted her headphones over her ears and then we were jolted forward, speeding and twisting through the underground tunnel upward until the pod came to a sudden stop. I noticed JJ looking a bit peaky.

"I hate this thing," he wheezed, gripping the sides of his seat.

"Aren't you used to going superfast?"

"Yeah, but when I can control it," he said, taking deep breaths. "It's unnatural to hurtle through tunnels underground."

The slabs of pavement lowered to our level, before lifting us back into fresh air and beautiful sunshine. I heard a loud scream as we magically appeared from beneath the ground. Looking for the source, I realized that a crowd of tourists was gathered around the Richard I statue in the front courtyard of the Houses of Parliament and every one of them was staring at us.

"Nothing to see here!" I said, attempting a cheery tone. "Wow, look at that great statue! It must have a fascinating history!"

"Aurora," Cherry said suddenly, lowering her headphones back around her neck. "It was difficult to make much out when I was on the Superhero Express, but there were definitely people in that underground complex who are not in the main conference room. I could hear their footsteps."

"It may have been Aunt Lucinda and Alfred."

She shook her head. "No, Alfred's ostrich footsteps are very distinctive; I know which ones were theirs. There were others."

"Wait," JJ said, holding up his hands and trying to ignore the tourists now taking pictures of us. "Others? Plural? You mean…"

"I think whoever has stolen the Light of the World isn't working alone." Cherry gulped.

"OK," I nodded, attempting to stay calm. "That's good to know. They all have to come up this way sometime, right? And we'll be ready for them."

"Lightning Girl?" A voice squeaked behind me.

I spun round to see a woman smiling nervously at me.

"Can we have a picture with you?" she asked, nodding toward her group of friends who were shuffling toward us with their phones.

I was just about to launch into a hurried explanation about how I didn't exactly have *time* to pose for photos right now because I was in the middle of stopping a load of bad guys from getting away with the most precious stone on the PLANET, but as I opened my mouth to speak, we were all suddenly distracted by a loud whirring noise coming from the sky.

There were cries and gasps of amazement as everyone looked upward, squinting against the sun.

"What is *that*?"

"That," I squeaked, barely able to contain my excitement, "is NANNY BEAM!"

Hovering above our heads was a sleek, bright-pink sports car, preparing to land right in front of the Houses of Parliament. The crowds parted as it came lower and lower, parking itself neatly next to the Richard I statue. The engine switched off and the driver's door opened upward, revealing a cheerful

elderly woman with matching pink hair.

"Nanny Beam!" I cried.

"Hello, Aurora," she waved cheerily, pretending not to notice everyone staring wide-eyed at her. "You may have noticed the invisibility function isn't working. Must work on that. Anyway, thought you might need some backup."

She climbed out of the car and opened the rear door. I saw a blur of fur pelting toward me before it leapt on me, causing me to stumble backward.

"Kimmy!" I laughed, as my dog covered my face in licks. "I am so happy to see you!"

"I know a flying car is cool and everything,"

I heard a voice say as someone else emerged from the back seat, "but next time I am not sitting next to Fred. He hogs the armrest."

"Well, maybe next time you can stop yourself from dousing yourself in hair spray right before you get in the car. You practically suffocated me. And at least you didn't get your eye almost poked out by one of Georgie's knitting needles."

"It is not a *knitting* needle, Fred. I was *sewing*! And it wasn't my fault that Kizzy's books were taking up so much room that when we took that right turn through the cloud, they jolted my arm."

"Those books are necessary for research and I couldn't fit them in the front seat with me when I already had all the chickens in the footwell."

JJ and Cherry turned to look at me in confusion.

"Aurora," JJ asked, "who are these people?"

"JJ and Cherry," I grinned, "meet the Bright Sparks!"

I raced toward Suzie, Fred, Georgie and Kizzy, pulling them into a big group hug. Kimmy jumped up and down at my legs, barking happily.

"Ow, Aurora!" Suzie grumbled, although she was smiling as she said it. "Watch my hair."

"What are you all *doing* here?" I asked, feeling as though I might burst into tears at the relief of seeing them.

"Nanny Beam came to get us," Kizzy explained. "We all saw the news and were working out how to all get to London to help you in time. Then Nanny Beam appeared out of nowhere. She picked each of us up."

"We knew that there was no way that it was you who had stolen the Light of the World from the conference," Georgie said firmly.

I smiled, squeezing Kizzy's hand as she nodded in agreement with Georgie. "I knew you would believe me. Aunt Lucinda and Alfred helped me escape, along with JJ and Cherry."

JJ and Cherry waved as the Bright Sparks all turned to look at them.

"Where's the Light of the World now?" Nanny Beam asked seriously.

"We don't know, and we don't know who has it. But" – I pointed at the lamppost – "whoever it is must emerge from there at some time. We planned to stop them as they tried to get away. Well, if they haven't already."

"Emerge from ... the lamppost?" Suzie said, raising her eyebrows at me.

"Actually it's a door. It's a long story."

"Aurora, we know who has the Light of the World," Kizzy announced.

"What? How can you possibly—"

"As soon as the news broke on social media about the Superhero Conference taking place here in London and that the Light of the World had been stolen by you... Well, Alexis got straight to work," she said, getting out her phone and pressing a button to make a video call. "He wants to speak to you."

Kizzy held up the screen of her phone for me and my brother waved from his desk in his bedroom.

"Hey, loser," Alexis grinned, positioning his phone on the desk so that he could type while speaking to me. "Any chance you can go a day or two without causing a national disaster?"

"I didn't take the Light of the World!" I said, grabbing the phone and frowning at the camera.

"Duh. As if you're that genius. But lucky for you, I know who is."

"You do?"

"I traced the IP address of the laptop that leaked the stories about the conference to the press. I figured that whoever wanted to point the finger at you, wanted it pointed away from themselves."

"And you managed to track who the laptop belonged to?" I asked urgently.

"Yep," Alexis nodded. "In just a few seconds."

"Who is it? Darek Vermore?" I asked.

Alexis frowned. "Darek Vermore? Why would you think it was him? No way, he's an icon. You know, he developed his first computer program at the age of four and—"

"If it's not him," I interrupted, "then who could it be?"

"I've never heard the name before. Someone called … David Donnelly."

JJ's jaw dropped to the floor.

"*What*?" I shook my head at the phone. "That can't be right. David Donnelly is just an assistant, he's not even a superhero. He's really nice. Are you sure it's not Vermore?"

"The leak came from David Donnelly's laptop, Aurora," Alexis said stubbornly. "Whoever you think he is, he isn't."

"But, why would David Donnelly do that?" Cherry asked, turning to JJ who looked as baffled as she was. "He seemed so … harmless."

"Well, I managed to hack into his laptop and he had copies of blueprints of the conference center on there, along with stolen notes on the vault and safe mechanisms." Alexis folded his arms and leaned back in his chair. "Trust me, he's a bad guy."

"Hang on," Georgie said suddenly, grabbing my arm. "LOOK!"

She pointed at the lamppost and we spun round just as the paving slabs opened and David Donnelly emerged from the ground, wearing a huge backpack AND a satchel round his shoulders.

"Thanks for the heads-up, Alexis. I've got to go," I said, passing Kizzy her phone back.

"Go save the world, loser," I heard Alexis say before hanging up. I'm almost certain that he sounded quite proud when he said it.

David Donnelly froze as he saw us all staring at him. Kimmy began growling loudly at him as soon as she laid eyes on him. She has always had a good instinct.

"It's him! *David Donnelly*!" I cried. "He's

got the Light of the World!"

"No, no! You've got it all wrong!" he croaked, edging backward and glancing nervously at Kimmy. "I don't have it! I … I came up here to help you find the culprit!"

As he turned on his heel, about to run away from us, Kimmy pounced, knocking him to the ground, his glasses scattering across the pavement. She then gripped his hair in her jaws and pulled. His mop of hair came clean off, revealing his shiny bald head.

"A wig!" Cherry exclaimed as Kimmy spat it on the ground. "It's a disguise!"

"Who are you?" JJ yelled.

David Donnelly turned to look up at us from the ground. "I suppose there's no need to hide it from you any longer."

His Scottish accent had vanished. And I recognized that voice. A familiar, menacing, thin-lipped smile crept across his face. He lifted a hand and slowly peeled off a very realistic fake nose.

"It *can't* be," Kizzy whispered.

I shook my head in utter disbelief.

"*Mr. Mercury*," I gasped.

"Hello, Aurora," he cackled, getting to his feet. "It's been far too long. Have you missed me?"

16

It couldn't be. It just couldn't be. I rubbed my eyes, but no matter how many times I blinked, Mr. Mercury was still there standing in front of me.

"You're supposed to be in prison," Fred croaked.

"You didn't hear? I was set free," Mr. Mercury said smugly.

Kizzy scowled. "Escaped, more like," she said. "How did you do it?"

"I'm disappointed you think so lowly of your

old science teacher, Kizzy. I did no such thing. I was released fair and square … with a little help from some old friends, of course." He sniggered.

"The same friends who employed you to steal the precious stones from the Natural History Museum?" Kizzy asked.

"I couldn't say," he said, shrugging.

"You've been under my nose this whole time," I said, shaking my head. "How could I not have noticed?"

"Yes, well, I know someone who works in a theater props department and he was only too happy to show off about how to master the art of disguise. I picked up some excellent tips and became shy, clumsy David Donnelly very easily."

"How did you con your way into the conference?" Suzie asked. "You'd never pass as a superhero, no matter what your disguise."

"I could too," he growled irritably. "But for ease, I saw that Darek Vermore was hiring a new assistant. It was the perfect way in without attracting suspicion." He smirked. "It was an added bonus that when the Light of the World was stolen, the blame fell on you, Aurora. I have been longing for revenge since you, your friends and that pesky ostrich put me behind bars."

"All right, that's enough," Nanny Beam said, stepping forward. "Hand over the Light of the World, Mr. Mercury, and tell us who you are working for. There's no way of outrunning us, not when JJ is here."

JJ blinked at her, stunned. "You … you know about my powers?"

"Running? *Running?*" Mr. Mercury cackled loudly before she could answer. "Oh, Nanny Beam, how quaint you are. I won't be running anywhere. I'll be … FLYING!"

He reached behind him and tugged on one of his backpack's toggles. The cloth of his backpack fell away, revealing a high-tech jet pack.

"The Rocket-750!" Nanny Beam gasped. "The latest model. How did you get your hands on one of those?"

"My *friends* are very generous," he said. "So long, Bright Sparks! Until next time!"

As he reached to press a button on his jet pack, I tried to muster my powers to work, but I was too panicked and caught off guard to focus properly.

"He's going to get away!" I cried, as flames billowed behind him.

"Not on our watch!" Fred bellowed. "Suzie, catch!"

Out of his backpack, he drew a thin white stick attached to a long piece of bright-pink ribbon and threw it toward Suzie. She caught the gymnastics ribbon perfectly and with a sharp flick of her wrist, twirled the ribbon swiftly through the air in a neat spiral above her head, before sending it flying in Mr. Mercury's direction just as he was propelled into the air.

The ribbon wrapped itself around Mr. Mercury and his jet pack, stopping him with a sharp jolt.

"Perfect, Suzie!" Georgie cried, addressing our gobsmacked audience. "Two-time Nationals winner, everyone!"

"I won the Nationals *three* times in a row," Suzie corrected.

Mr. Mercury roared with anger, trying his best to break free of the ribbon coiled around him, as Suzie tried with all her might to pull him back to earth.

"He's too strong!" she yelled, gripping the handle tightly and digging her heels into the ground. "My hands are slipping!"

"Here, let me," JJ said, taking the gymnastics ribbon out of her grip.

Suzie's eyes widened in awe as, with seemingly no effort whatsoever, JJ pulled the ribbon sharply back toward him, and Mr. Mercury came tumbling down to earth, his jet pack landing on the pavement with a loud clunk.

Wobbling to his feet, Mr. Mercury tried pressing the button on his jet pack, but it spluttered, letting out black plumes of smoke, before cutting out altogether.

"No!" he shouted, pressing the button again and again. "Work! Argh!"

He furiously wriggled out of the jet pack and threw it to the ground, before turning on his heel to make a beeline for Nanny Beam's supercar.

"JJ, quick!" Cherry yelled. "Don't let him get away."

But it turned out there was no need for JJ to run after Mr. Mercury because Nanny Beam was ready and waiting behind him.

Bellowing a karate battle shout at the top of her lungs, Nanny Beam did an incredible high kick, knocking Mr. Mercury sideways.

"Whoa!" Fred cried. "Go, Nanny Beam!"

Mr. Mercury regained his balance and narrowed his eyes at Nanny Beam, lifting his clenched fists and moving into a prepared, forward stance.

"You've met your match, Nanny Beam," he growled threateningly. "I'm no stranger to the martial arts!"

To support his point, he began to dance on his toes around her, showcasing his head-level kicks and swinging his elbows, just missing her jaw. She dodged and defended, blocking any blows he threw at her, but there was no denying that Mr. Mercury was actually very good and a lot stronger than her. JJ ran over to help, but Mr. Mercury spun round and sharply struck him in the stomach, winding him badly, before he turned his attention back to Nanny Beam.

"Aurora," Kizzy said, clutching my arm, "use your superpowers to stop him before he hurts Nanny Beam! The energy blast might stun him and we can get his bag."

"I … I can't," I replied, wincing as Nanny Beam just managed to duck another kick. "I've lost most of the ability!"

"No, you haven't."

"Yes, Kizzy, I have," I told her desperately. "I've let the Bright Sparks down. I'm not a superhero anymore! Just look online. It says so."

"I don't need to look online; I know a superhero when I see one," Kizzy said stubbornly.

"You *are* Lightning Girl and you always will be to us, no matter what anyone else says," Georgie said, as Kizzy nodded vigorously. "Here."

Georgie reached into her pocket and pulled out a pair of sunglasses. All around the frames were tiny glittering lightning bolts.

"Where did you—"

"I designed them for you. For Lightning Girl," she said, holding them out for me to put on. "I know Alfred destroyed yours. Why would I go to the trouble of making these if I didn't think you deserved them?"

"Come on, Lightning Girl," Kizzy said urgently. "Everyone needs you."

I don't know whether it was what Georgie

and Kizzy were saying or if it was the way they were looking at me, but something happened as I took the sunglasses and put them on. The Bright Sparks were counting on me and they believed in me, even if no one else did.

"You can do this." Kizzy smiled encouragingly.

I forgot about all the times I'd messed up; I didn't think about the *Good Morning Britain* disaster or the upside-down-ladder incident or how silly I'd felt in the superhero training room. All I was focused on was that wonderfully warm sparkling feeling running through my veins, up my spine and down my arms toward my hands, which grew hot. The swirled scar on my palm began to prickle and a silver glow appeared around the outline of my fingers.

The crowd suddenly gasped as Nanny Beam

was struck in the chest by Mr. Mercury and went flying backward.

You can do this, Kizzy's voice echoed in my head.

Go save the world, I heard Alexis saying.

"Unlucky, Bright Sparks," Mr. Mercury said, throwing open the front door of Nanny Beam's pink car. "Say goodbye to the Light of the World!"

You can do this, Lightning Girl.

Light beams exploded from my palms, basking the Houses of Parliament and all those around it in a blinding, glittering light. It happened with such force that Mr. Mercury stumbled backward, shielding his eyes and then crying out as Kimmy — who had chased him to the car, barking madly — tucked herself neatly behind his feet, causing him to lose his balance and tumble back over her, landing with a thud on the ground.

As I brought my powers under control and the light faded, I saw everyone staring at me in amazement. Nanny Beam wiped a tear from her eye.

"GERROFF ME!"

We all turned to see that Mr. Mercury was pinned to the ground by Alfred, who had come from nowhere and was now standing on Mr. Mercury, pecking at his bald head.

"I HATE THIS OSTRICH!" Mr. Mercury bellowed, his arms and legs flailing about wildly.

"I LOVE that ostrich!" Georgie cried out.

The crowd who had witnessed the whole thing burst into applause and cheering, chanting "Lightning Girl" over and over. Alfred plucked the satchel from Mr. Mercury and chucked it toward me.

I opened it and peered inside, my breath catching in my throat as I saw the contents.

"Aurora?" Nanny Beam said, joining the Bright Sparks who gathered around me. "What's wrong?"

"It's … it's empty," I croaked. "The Light of the World isn't here."

Underneath Alfred's talons, Mr. Mercury began to cackle manically.

"*Where is it?*" Nanny Beam demanded.

But he didn't need to answer. As she spoke,

a helicopter took off from the other side of the Houses of Parliament.

"Mr. Mercury was just a decoy," Kizzy gasped.

"That's right! We've won this time," Mr. Mercury boasted gleefully. "And I can promise you this, Bright Sparks. I will NEVER tell you who I was working for!"

Suddenly, a shiny silver sports car with blacked-out windows pulled up on the pavement next to us, its brakes screeching loudly as it came to a stop. One of the front windows wound down and a hand protruded out of it, a beautiful diamond necklace dangling from a finger.

Alfred's eyes lit up.

"ALFRED, NO!" I cried, but it was too late.

He had already jumped off Mr. Mercury and pelted toward the car. Whoever was holding the necklace tossed it high into the air for Alfred to catch, while Mr. Mercury, no longer

weighed down by
a large ostrich, scrambled
to his feet, dodged past Kizzy and
leapt into the back seat of the car before any
of us could realize what was happening.

The door slammed shut behind Mr. Mercury,
the engine roared as the accelerator pedal was
slammed to the floor and the car sped away
down the road, disappearing from sight.

I could hear the menacing sound of Mr.
Mercury's cackle echoing through the air as
I helplessly watched it go.

17

"AURORA!"

I jumped about fifteen feet in the air as I heard my name echo loudly, booming off the walls of the underground dome, before I was quite literally swept off my feet into the biggest hug I have ever had. Kimmy began barking and jumping up and down in excitement.

"Mum," I wheezed, "I … can't … breathe!"

"Oh, sorry!" she said, breaking free from the hug but keeping her hands on my shoulders. "Are you all right?"

"Yes, although next time, maybe don't squeeze so hard. I think you may have cracked a couple of my ribs."

"I'm not talking about the hug! I'm talking about us being trapped down here and you being left alone to stop the thief up there!"

She pointed to the ceiling.

"Oh that! Yeah, I'm OK and I wasn't alone."

She nodded, tears in her eyes, and stepped aside so that Dad, who came rushing up behind her, could give me another rib-crushing hug. Meanwhile, Kimmy jumped up at Mum to cover her face in licks.

"We were so worried," Dad said, pushing his glasses up his nose. "We were completely trapped in that conference room; the whole thing was superhero-proof! No contact with the outside world, no idea what was going on, no idea whether you would be safe..." He paused for breath. "It was awful."

"I'm all right, Dad. I had reinforcements," I assured him, gesturing to the Bright Sparks who were sitting around the fountain with Crystal, asking her over and over to disappear, gasping every time she turned invisible.

The Bright Sparks had been given special permission by Nanny Beam to come down to the Superhero Conference center. Fred had loved the Superhero Express and had his arms up in the air the whole time, going "WOOHOO" loudly at every twist and turn, irritating Suzie, who claimed as it came to a stop at the platform that he'd burst her eardrums.

Dad looked over his shoulder at them and smiled.

"Now, how on earth did they get here?"

"Tell us everything that happened," Mum said, her expression serious.

So I did. I told her how Aunt Lucinda and Alfred had come to my rescue, along with Cherry and JJ; how we'd realized what was going on, so we'd raced up above ground to beat the thief before they escaped; how the Bright Sparks and Alexis had worked out who the culprit was; and how in the end, I had failed.

"Failed?" Mum held up her hands, stopping my story. "What do you mean?"

"Mum, they got away," I said, patting Kimmy's head as she came to sit next to me, leaning against my leg. "We don't have the Light of the World."

"That doesn't mean you *failed*," she said, shaking her head.

"If you hadn't been brave enough to try and stop Mr. Mercury, we'd have no clue where to start when it comes to tracking down the Light of the World," Dad pointed out. "We know that Mr. Mercury is somehow involved. That's a good start. Along with the police, we can do everything in our power to try and discover where he is and who he is working for."

"But aren't we in a lot of danger?" I asked. "The Light of the World is the most precious stone there is and the source of our powers. In the wrong hands, couldn't something awful happen?"

Mum and Dad exchanged a worried glance.

Dad nodded. "Yes, Aurora, you're right. We don't know what this criminal mastermind wants with the Light of the World. But the important thing is that you're safe and we're all together."

"Dad's right," Mum said, reaching for his hand and smiling up at him. "Whoever it is, they won't be a match for the Beams and the Bright Sparks."

Kimmy barked loudly.

"I suppose if Kimmy says so," I agreed, stroking her ears.

"There you are, darling!" Aunt Lucinda called out, sauntering over to us with Alfred trotting along behind her.

"Isn't it simply marvelous how we saved the day! There Kiyana was, trapped in a conference room while the thieves got away and who came along to rescue her and set her free? Why, her glamorous and talented younger twin sister!"

Mum rolled her eyes. "I'm never going to hear the end of this, am I?"

"Not for several years at least." Aunt Lucinda grinned, winking at me. "That control room was particularly tricky as well; I had no idea how to turn off the security lockdown at first. When I saw all those buttons on the security panel, I felt quite faint! But luckily, Alfred was there to show the quickest, most effective way of hitting the right one."

"How did he do it?" Dad asked curiously. "Some kind of elimination process?"

Aunt Lucinda laughed. "You might say that," she said. "He hopped up onto the control panel and began stomping all over it. Eventually, he must have hit the correct button. Such a clever ostrich."

Alfred, who had found a long red cape and was wearing it with pride, wiggled his tail feathers smugly.

"*What?*" Mum gasped. "He could have pressed anything, Lucinda!"

"Indeed, he did, Kiyana. He actually set off several more alarms before turning off the right one and lifting the lockdown. At one point, he hit a button that said 'self-destruct' in bold letters across it, but luckily he hit another one which deactivated it."

Mum and Dad looked horrified.

"I'm just grateful Alfred came to help us when he did," I said, trying to steer the conversation into a more positive direction. "Even if Mr. Mercury got away in the end, it was still satisfying to see Alfred pecking at his head."

"Yes, I'd wondered where Alfred had gotten to after we found the right button, but I should have guessed he'd gone above ground." Aunt Lucinda chuckled. "He absolutely loves the Superhero Express. I imagine he was rewarding himself for finding the button with a ride in one of those pods, when he spotted what was going on with you and rushed to your aid. Although, he's very disappointed that the diamond necklace he was distracted with was fake. I thought I had taught him better." She hesitated. "I can't believe it was Mr. Mercury *again*."

"And he was here all along in disguise. I felt bad for David Donnelly," Dad grumbled. "I even lent him my book on advanced mineralogy. I doubt I'll ever get that book back now. And I hadn't even finished the chapter on mineralogical geothermobarometry."

We all stared at him in silence as he shook

his head gravely.

"Er, yes, Henry. Well don't worry, we can order you another copy of that ... fascinating book," Mum said soothingly.

"It's all right," he said. "I'll just borrow Clara's copy when she's finished with it."

"HEY!" JJ cried as he noticed Alfred from where he was sitting with his parents. "THAT'S MY CAPE!"

We all burst out laughing as JJ began to chase Alfred – who looked delighted with the situation – round and round the fountain. Despite JJ's super speed, Alfred's long legs were quite a match.

"Kiyana and I do owe you and Alfred for coming to help Aurora," Dad admitted to Aunt Lucinda, chuckling as Alfred galloped through the fountain and watching JJ stomp in after him, getting soaked in the process. The Bright Sparks cheered them on loudly.

"As soon as I saw the ridiculous accusations about Aurora taking the precious stone on the news, there was no question about Alfred and me attending the Superhero Conference." Aunt Lucinda smiled. "Plus, I was wondering whether I might be able to get away with stealing it myself."

Mum narrowed her eyes at her. "I *know* you're not joking."

"Please do feel free to thank me for saving your daughter, Kiyana," Aunt Lucinda continued smugly. "Whenever you're ready."

Mum appealed to Dad, but he just gave her a stern look.

"Thank you," she said eventually, through gritted teeth.

"You are most welcome," Aunt Lucinda replied, before adding, "I will send you a bill for my services."

Mum opened her mouth to say something,

but her phone beeped loudly in her pocket.

"How ... how are you getting mobile service here?" I asked, baffled.

"I don't know." She pulled out her phone, her eyebrows knitted in confusion. "I haven't had any since I've been down here. I don't know how this message has..."

She stopped, blinking at her screen in amazement.

"What?" I asked eagerly. "What is it?"

"It's ... it's my source," she said quietly, as though hardly daring to say it out loud. "My secret source from the British Secret Service."

"They need you to go on a superhero mission *now*?" Dad said. "Haven't they seen the news? They must know you're busy."

She shook her head. "They don't want me to go on a mission. They want to *meet* me. They're here. In the Superhero Conference. They say that it's time."

"WHERE?" I practically screamed, I was so excited.

"They've said to come to Mr. Vermore's office."

"What are we waiting for?" I cried, grabbing her hand. "Let's go!"

"What's going on?" Aunt Lucinda called out after us as I dragged Mum away, with Dad in hot pursuit. "Kiyana! Where are you going?"

We didn't stop to answer her, rushing through the spaceship door and down the maze of corridors that led to Mr. Vermore's office. When we got there, stopping to catch our breath, we saw that the door was slightly ajar.

"This is it," Mum whispered, grabbing Dad's hand nervously. "I'm finally going to meet them. After all these years of secrecy, I'm finally going to meet the person in charge of it all."

Dad nodded encouragingly at her and I stood aside to let her open the door and go in first ... you know, because I kind of felt she should probably lead the way, even though I was desperate to burst right on in.

Mum took a deep breath and rolled back her shoulders, before pushing open the door and striding into the office confidently. Dad and I followed anxiously.

A large leather chair behind an antique mahogany desk was facing away from us.

"You ... you wanted to meet me?" Mum said cautiously to the back of the chair.

"Yes. Yes, I did," a voice said.

The chair slowly swiveled round. Mum gasped as she saw who it was. Dad's jaw dropped to the floor. I could NOT believe my eyes.

No. Way.

"Hello, Kiyana." Nanny Beam smiled from the chair, stroking a chicken nestled in her lap. "I've been expecting you."

Mum looked as though she'd seen a ghost.

She stood frozen to the spot, staring at Nanny Beam with her eyes wide in shock and her mouth opening and closing silently like a fish as she tried to form words.

"Yes, Kiyana," Nanny Beam said, tickling the chin of the chicken on her lap, prompting it to cluck happily. "It is me, Nanny Beam."

Mum still didn't seem to be in a fit state to speak, so Dad jumped in. "You're Kiyana's source?" he asked in disbelief.

Nanny Beam nodded.

"But … *how*?"

"That's a very good question, Henry. And one with a very simple answer. It's about time you knew. I have been working for the Secret Intelligence Service since my early twenties."

"You're a spy?" I squeaked, finding it difficult not to jump up and down on the spot with excitement.

"Technically, yes."

My grandmother is a spy.

MY GRANDMOTHER IS A SPY.

THIS IS THE COOLEST THING EVER.

"It was *you*?"

We all turned to look at Mum as she managed to finally find her voice.

"Yes, Kiyana. It was me. I've been anonymously sending you on rescue missions to stop evil taking over the world for years.

In my government position, I have access to the equipment and information necessary to know when a dangerous individual is a threat. And that's where you came in."

"But … but you're retired!" Mum croaked, trying to get her head round all this. "You have a stray chicken sanctuary in Cornwall! You can't possibly work for MI5! None of this makes sense!"

"Oh yes, my animal sanctuary is a very important part of my life, but by no means my only occupation. I may have retired from saving the world physically, but I haven't retired from saving the world altogether." She grinned. "A truth that Aurora stumbled upon this summer."

Mum and Dad turned their attention to me.

"Aurora found my underground lair and I was forced to admit that I still had a hand in the game, as it were," Nanny Beam explained, lifting the chicken off her lap and tucking him under her arm so she could stand up.

"You didn't tell me you were a SPY!"

She shrugged and let out a long sigh. "Yes, well, I wasn't planning on *ever* telling you that I was the head of the Secret Intelligence Service, but now that the Light of the World is in danger, I decided it was time that you knew, so we could all work together."

"Hold on." Dad held up his hands. "Did you just say ... the *head* of the Secret Intelligence Service?"

"Did I not mention that already?" Nanny Beam said, her brow furrowed in thought. "Oh, must have missed that detail. Yes, yes, I'm in charge."

"My grandmother who has pink hair, stray chickens and spends her time Sun Gazing is the head of MI5," I whispered. "Am I dreaming?

Is this really happening?"

Now the whole underground lair thing TOTALLY made sense.

"How else would I be able to know where and when to send Kiyana on superhero missions?" Nanny Beam said breezily. "I know everything."

"I don't believe this," Mum said, her stunned expression changing to anger. "You told me you were RETIRED! And the whole time you were the HEAD OF MI5! Spying on me!"

Nanny Beam sighed. "It's hardly something you shout about, Kiyana. And besides, I wasn't the head of MI5 the *whole* time. Just for the past ten or so years. I had to work my way up, of course. I believed it to be a very savvy career choice, once I learned about my superpowers. How better to keep an eye on the world and make sure I was always there to save it than within the Secret Intelligence Service?

The resources at our fingertips are quite spectacular."

"And then when you gave up the superpowers, you used your position to spy on your daughter," Mum growled.

"Don't be ridiculous," Nanny Beam tutted. "As if I would ever give up my superpowers. But yes, it was time for me to retire from the physical side of things and let you step into that role. Although, I'm pleased to inform you that my martial arts skills aren't as rusty as I thought they'd be after all these years, as your Mr. Mercury can attest to."

"Didn't you trust me to save the world on my own?" Mum was practically yelling. "You didn't have faith in my ability, so you never retired, is that it?"

Nanny Beam stared at Mum very calmly. "No, Kiyana, that's not it. I just wasn't ready to retire from MI5 quite yet, and besides, wasn't it easier getting all that information about bad guys? You have to admit it saved you a lot of time, not having to seek them out. You're a wonderful superhero, even better than me I might add."

She hesitated and her eyes flickered toward me, twinkling with excitement.

"Although, Kiyana, you should have seen Aurora today when she used her powers. It was like nothing I've ever seen. There is something truly special about—"

"Mother, don't change the subject!" Mum cried out in exasperation. "Why haven't you told me any of this sooner? You've been lying to me!"

"I wasn't allowed to tell you," Nanny Beam answered simply. "MI5 is very cagey about these things. James Bond hardly went around blabbing about his job description. Anyway, I've told you now. You know my secret."

The room fell into silence. Dad was looking at Mum worriedly as she leaned on the desk and just shook her head at Nanny Beam.

"Well," Dad said brightly, clearing his throat, "I guess it's not every day that you find out your mother-in-law is the most powerful intelligence officer in Britain, eh? I had better watch my step!"

He chuckled and Mum narrowed her eyes at him.

"But … er … the most important thing to remember here is that we're family and, despite our … um, secrets, we have to stick together," he said hurriedly. "Right, Kiyana?"

Mum inhaled deeply. "I suppose."

"Right, Nanny Beam?"

"Right, Henry." She smiled warmly at Kiyana. "You've made me very proud all these years."

The corner of Mum's mouth twitched as she tried and failed to suppress a smile.

At that moment, the door burst open behind us and Darek Vermore barreled in, followed closely by Aunt Lucinda and Alfred, still wearing his new cape. I giggled, thinking of poor JJ.

"Ah, Darek!" Nanny Beam said, beckoning him over. "I've been wondering where you'd gotten to."

Nanny Beam put the chicken on the floor; it immediately stalked over to cluck at Alfred.

"Sorry, Nanny Beam," he spluttered, running a hand through his hair. "I've just been checking that all the superheroes are OK and the security systems are back up and running."

"What's going on in here?" Aunt Lucinda demanded. "Kiyana, why did you run away like that? The Bright Sparks are wondering where everyone has gotten to, not to mention an entire conference of superheroes."

"Is it true?" Mr. Vermore asked Nanny

Beam, ignoring Aunt Lucinda. "What they're saying about David?"

"Yes. Your assistant, David Donnelly, was actually the notorious Mr. Mercury in disguise. He was working for someone else this whole time. But I'm afraid whoever he was working for made off with the Light of the World in one of your helicopters and Mr. Mercury got away too, with their help."

Mr. Vermore sunk down into the chair that Nanny Beam had occupied before. He buried his head in his hands.

"So David Donnelly was behind all this," he groaned. "He had access to everything."

I felt guilty seeing him so disheartened. I'd been so distracted by the idea of Darek Vermore being behind everything, I hadn't even looked twice at David Donnelly.

I clenched my fists thinking how easily I fell into Mr. Mercury's trap.

"Mr. Mercury worked out how to break into the safe," Nanny Beam continued. "No doubt by hacking your personal files. He also knew how to put on a complete lockdown of the conference room, trapping all the superheroes so they couldn't stop him. Quite genius, really."

Mr. Vermore nodded and then lifted his gaze to meet mine. "I'm so sorry for thinking it might be you, Aurora. I really believed though, that if you had taken it, you were just trying to protect it. Either way I knew you wouldn't have wanted it for selfish reasons. I apologize for locking you in your room."

"Don't worry about it," I said hurriedly, as he smiled back. "I actually thought it was you who had taken it, so we're both guilty of that mistake."

"But I let you down, Nanny Beam." He sighed miserably. "I promised you that the precious stone would be safe here during the conference."

"Hold on, you two *know* each other?" Mum asked, wiggling her finger at Mr. Vermore and her mother.

"Ah, yes, I should explain," Nanny Beam began. "One more secret you should know."

"What do you mean, one *more* secret?" Aunt Lucinda asked, raising her eyebrows. "What did I miss?"

"Can we tell her?" I asked Nanny Beam excitedly.

"Go ahead."

"Nanny Beam is the head of the Secret Intelligence Service," I explained to Aunt Lucinda, who blinked at me.

"I beg your pardon?"

"Our mother has been working for MI5 all our lives and now she runs the department," Mum added, pursing her lips. "Just a tiny family secret she revealed moments before your arrival."

Aunt Lucinda turned to look at Nanny Beam who nodded back at her. Alfred, who had been distracted by the chicken, snapped his head up on hearing this news and peered closely at Nanny Beam, before bowing dramatically at her feet.

"Thank you, Alfred," she chuckled. "No need for that."

"So, what could possibly be the other secret you have to tell us?" Mum asked curiously.

Nanny Beam and Mr. Vermore exchanged a glance before Nanny Beam cleared her throat, addressing Mum and Aunt Lucinda.

"There was a reason that a few years ago, I asked Mr. Vermore here to come on board as the official sponsor of any superhero conferences that would be held in the future. In my capacity as the head of SIS, he had my full support to build this extraordinary complex and host our superhero activity here. I felt safe in the knowledge that he understood our powers and our superhero nature a little better than others." She hesitated. "And the reason I knew that was because he is, in fact, my nephew. Kiyana, Lucinda, meet your cousin, Darek."

Mr. Vermore gave them an awkward wave.

"Hi, cousins!" he said enthusiastically. "I think the Beam superpowers are AWESOME. I wish I had them."

"Wait a second," I gasped as something suddenly clicked in my head. "It's YOU! From the photo!"

He gave me a strange look. "I'm sorry? Are you talking about my commercials?"

"No, no, I knew I recognized you the first time we met. I thought it was from the television, but something else was bothering me," I explained. "At Nanny Beam's I saw an old photo of her with her brother. And the little boy in the photo was *you*!"

"Yes, Darek is the son of my brother, and although things between my sibling and me..." Nanny Beam paused, looking tense, and Darek stared at his feet. "Well, never mind. Anyway, Darek has always stayed in touch and is fully aware of the Beam women's heritage. I have watched his business ambition blossom with interest and when I thought it was suitable, I introduced him to the superhero world and brought him on as the sponsor. As Darek was under orders not to let the nature of my job be known, he wasn't able to inform you of the family connection. But, there you have it."

Nanny Beam patted Darek gently on the shoulder.

"Your father and I had our differences, but I know that he would have been very proud of you," she said quietly to him. He beamed at her.

"Wow!" Dad exclaimed when nobody else said anything. "This is quite a day!"

"I'm so excited to get to know you both properly, as family," Darek beamed. "And you, Aurora and Henry, of course. But I'm afraid I must dash. The press is swarming the Houses of Parliament, trying to get the lowdown on what happened, and their attempts to find the entrance to the conference are causing a bit of hassle. Apparently, one of the reporters has been arrested for climbing the statue of Richard I and clubbing it with his shoe."

Nanny Beam chuckled. "How inventive. Off you go, Darek, and do some crowd control. I'll take care of everything here."

"Oh, before I go," Darek said, stopping at the door and addressing Mum and Dad, "I hear that your eldest, Alexis, is very talented when it comes to technology?"

"That's right," I nodded proudly. "He was the one who worked out that David Donnelly was bad news. He managed to track him down as the leak of all the stories to the press."

"I see." Darek smiled. "He sounds like exactly what I'm looking for in an intern. I'm always looking for the next star. Perhaps he'd like to spend a few weeks with me over Christmas break. My company deals with the latest in technology and, as you can see, we have a close relationship with the government, so get to work on some pretty cool projects. He could come learn the ropes and gain some experience, if he'd like. It's really the least I could do."

"I'm sure he'd love that," Dad gushed. "We'll pass on the message. Thank you, Mr. Vermore."

He waved happily at us before bustling

through the door and away down the corridor.

"As if *he* is your cousin. And a good guy!" Dad said, when he'd disappeared. "I thought that if anyone was suspicious, it was him!"

"Yes, Mr. Mercury had a stroke of luck with that," Nanny Beam agreed. "I hear that Darek was very stressed and snappy under the pressure of such responsibility. He distracted everyone from his dim-witted assistant."

"Darek Vermore is our cousin," Mum said under her breath. "*Cousin*! My mother is the head of the Secret Service."

"Well, I don't know about you, but I've had an overload of information and excitement for one day and could very much do with a hot chocolate," Dad said, nudging me.

"Yes. Me too!" I quickly agreed. "Let's go get the Bright Sparks and head home. We have *plenty* to talk about."

"Good idea," Mum said, looking very much

still in shock. "I'll call a taxi."

Dad put his arm round Mum and led her out. Aunt Lucinda sauntered along behind them while Alfred bent down so that the chicken could hop up onto his head and slide down his neck, nestling comfortably among Alfred's feathers.

"Hey, Nanny Beam," I whispered. "When do you think we should mention to Mum about your flying car?"

"Perhaps another time, Aurora," she laughed, throwing her arm around my shoulders. "I think she's had enough surprises for one day, don't you?"

The week before school started again, Nanny Beam invited the whole family and my friends to stay at her house in Cornwall and enjoy the last of the sunshine.

Along with the newest honorary additions to the Bright Sparks, of course.

Cherry smiled, sipping some coconut water from her perch on the roof. "I could get used to this," she said. "I wish this week didn't have to end. I want to stay here in the UK for a bit longer."

We'd spent the afternoon lounging up here after a session of Sun Gazing with Nanny Beam. Suzie had been loving the practice so much that she'd announced earlier that she had decided to petition for Sun Gazing sessions when we were back at school. Mum said that Nanny Beam had never looked prouder.

"The view is awesome," Georgie nodded, rubbing the belly of the alpaca lounging next to her before rearranging her towel across the tiles. "How are those sunglasses working out for you, Aurora?"

I pushed my Lightning Girl sunglasses up my nose. "They're the perfect fit."

She grinned. "Just you wait until you see what I've done with your school blazer. Those accessories are going to blow your mind."

"As long as they don't land me in detention."

"Oh, please," she laughed. "Haven't you heard? Nobody puts the mighty Lightning Girl in detention."

Since the showdown in front of the Houses of Parliament, my name had barely left the front page again. I was just glad that they were all saying nice things about Lightning Girl, now that my name had been cleared over the robbery of the Light of the World, but I was hoping that when I went back to school the attention would die down.

After all that had happened this summer, I had decided that there would be no more personal appearances, product launches or photo calls. And especially, no more breakfast television shows.

And since there wouldn't be a Lightning Girl schedule anymore, my PA felt there wasn't much for her to do and so handed in her resignation.

"I think I'll just stick to being your best friend," Kizzy had told me, deleting my calendar from her phone. "That's a full-time job in itself, what with us saving the world and stuff. Besides, someone needs to remind you how to work those powers of yours."

She may have been joking, but it turned out that Kizzy was right.

I'd ended up telling Mum all about how my powers wouldn't work in the superhero training room that time with JJ and Cherry, but then in front of the Houses of Parliament, they had come out in full force. She had listened to me carefully and then when I'd asked why that had happened, she'd just said, "Well, isn't it obvious?"

I'd told her no, it wasn't obvious, at least not to me.

"Aurora," Mum had smiled, her eyes boring into mine, "your powers are part of who you are. You had lost faith in yourself, which reflected in your superpowers. Kizzy and all the Bright Sparks showing up that day to be by your side and remind you to believe in yourself... Well, from what I hear, it caused those light beams to be more powerful and dazzling than ever."

I had been stunned at first, but the more I thought about it, the more it completely made sense.

Obviously, I couldn't tell the Bright Sparks about this, for ego reasons. Fred was already referring to himself as the Ultimate President of Crime Fighting to anyone who would listen.

He'd even had business cards made and was

handing them out on the Underground.

"Hey, guys, listen to this," Kizzy said enthusiastically from her spot on the corner of the roof. She cleared her throat and began to read aloud from the large book resting open in her lap.

"*Although cunning and resourceful, the notorious Blackout Burglar may not have been working alone. Detective Inspector Bumble, who worked on the Blackout Burglar's 1998 robbery of the famous Snowdrop Tiara — a priceless item belonging to Lady Camilla Camomile — stood firm to his belief that the Blackout Burglar had been financed by an unknown source, despite many officers declaring the detective 'doolally.' Without any evidence to support his theory, however, DI Bumble eventually gave up on the idea, quit the force a few years later and now runs a skateboarding business in Canada.*"

"What book is that?" Cherry asked, peering over her sunglasses at Kizzy.

"It's called *Crime, Criminals and Cat Burglars Through the Ages.* I got it out of the library for some light reading," she said. "Anyway, there's a whole section in here about Mr. Mercury."

"Sounds like that Detective Inspector Bumble might have been on to something," I said thoughtfully. "Mr. Mercury might have been working for the same person all those years ago when he was the Blackout Burglar."

"And whoever it is, it sounds like they're very powerful," Georgie pointed out. "They've been able to keep themselves out of his spotlight *and* they've been funding him the whole time."

"And now they've gotten their hands on the Light of the World," I grumbled, my heart sinking just like it did any time I thought about that helicopter flying away into the sunset.

"We'll stop them, Aurora," Kizzy said determinedly. "Nanny Beam said she's already on the case, tracking them down. If anyone can find them, it's Nanny Beam."

"Speaking of whom," Georgie laughed, nodding down toward the ground, "what do you think they're doing? Fred looks terrified."

Nanny Beam was standing with Fred, Suzie and JJ in the middle of the field next to the house. We couldn't hear what was going on as they were too far away, but Nanny Beam seemed to be barking orders at them and flinging her arms around a lot, while Fred's expression was full of worry. Kimmy had happily joined them in the field, along with some of her new alpaca friends, and was settling down in the grass to watch.

Cherry smiled, picking up her headphones and placing them over her ears. "I can tell you exactly what she's telling them," she said. "Give me a moment."

After a few minutes of concentrated listening,

she removed the headphones, sniggering.

"What?" Kizzy asked eagerly. "What is it?"

"Nanny Beam is teaching them some basic martial arts and, from the sounds of it, Fred isn't sure who he wants to go up against first: JJ or Suzie."

We all erupted into infectious giggles.

"It's a difficult choice," Kizzy laughed. "I mean, JJ does have super strength…"

"But have you seen Suzie right before a gymnastics competition?" Georgie said. "When she wants to be, she is *fierce*."

"And it looks like she's certainly a match for JJ," Cherry pointed out.

We watched Suzie swing her leg through the air in an impressive roundhouse kick. JJ ducked just in time, stumbling backward onto the grass, landing on his bottom. Nanny Beam gave Suzie a triumphant high five before ordering them all into a straight line so she could begin teaching them the next move.

"If I were Fred, I'd pick to go up against JJ," Kizzy said, and we all nodded along in agreement.

"Aurora! Are you up there?" Mum's voice called. "Can you come down for a minute?"

I left the others and climbed back through the roof hatch, down the ladder to where Mum was waiting for me.

"Aunt Lucinda is about to set off," she informed me. "I thought you'd want to say goodbye. She's in the kitchen."

I hurried down the stairs and found Aunt Lucinda sitting with my dad and Clara at the kitchen table.

"I'm telling you, Henry," Aunt Lucinda was saying tiredly, "why would you send your daughter to science camp next year when she can come learn how to rob banks with me? It only takes a few weeks to learn the knack, and taking into consideration Clara's superior intelligence, I'd say she'd be ready for her first shot at it in a matter of days."

Clara sniggered at Dad's horrified expression.

"There you are, Aurora," Aunt Lucinda said, standing up and pulling me into a hug. "Just in time to say toodle-loo!"

"Where are you off to this time?" I asked curiously. "Bora Bora? The Bahamas? Fiji?"

"Actually, I can't say," she said, tapping the side of her nose. "It's less of a vacation and more of a business trip. Mummy's orders."

"Nanny Beam is sending you on a mission?" Clara gasped. "Cool!"

"Yes, I suppose we must all play our part in finding where the Light of the World is and I'm hoping to squeeze in at least a *little* downtime," Aunt Lucinda replied.

"Nanny Beam will have her eye on you." Mum grinned, causing Aunt Lucinda to roll her eyes dramatically.

"Anyway, don't tell Alfred," Aunt Lucinda said hurriedly as we heard the familiar sound of Alfred's stomping coming down the stairs. "He doesn't do any work as a rule. It's his philosophy; he wouldn't come along with me if he knew. I'm having to pretend that we're going to the Great Barrier Reef."

Alfred suddenly appeared in the doorway of the kitchen wearing flippers, goggles and a snorkel.

"Oh good, darling, you're ready," Aunt Lucinda proclaimed loudly as Alfred hopped excitedly up and down in his flippers. "Let's get in the car, shall we?"

We followed them out to the driveway where Nanny

Beam's pink sports car was waiting, packed full of luggage. Aunt Lucinda slid into the driver's seat and pressed a button to let the roof down for Alfred.

"You're taking Nanny Beam's car?" I said in amazement.

"Yes, apparently she's working on a newer model anyway. Now that she's gotten the flying side of things down, she wants to improve it. And this invisibility function is faulty. Still, better than nothing." Aunt Lucinda turned the keys in the ignition and wiggled her fingers at Nanny Beam who was waving madly from the field. "As always, Beams, it's been a blast. Until next time!"

She pressed her foot down on the accelerator and zoomed off down the driveway, Alfred's head bobbing into the distance.

"Is it worrying that I think I may just miss your bonkers sister and her cantankerous ostrich a tiny bit?" Dad laughed, waving goodbye to them.

"Oh, she'll be back to cause trouble soon enough," Mum said with a sigh. "But I suppose things are a little more interesting when she's around."

"Where's Alexis?" Clara asked, shielding her eyes from the sun to look up at the roof. "I want to show him and Aurora my new book on geology."

"He's in the underground lair beneath the cottage, experimenting with all those computers. Nanny Beam has been teaching him some new tricks. I haven't been able to drag him away," Mum told her, rolling her eyes.

"Did Nanny Beam lend you your new geology book?" I asked Clara.

"Oh no," Dad said, puffing his chest out like a proud peacock and placing a hand on Clara's shoulder. "Clara *wrote* it."

"It's more like a pamphlet," Clara said hurriedly, shuffling her feet. "And it still needs some editing. Would you like to see it?"

"Are you kidding?" I laughed. "YES!"

"Come on, Clara," Dad said. "Let's go get it. We can grab Alexis on the way and force him into the sunlight."

They disappeared inside and while we waited, Mum and I strolled to the edge of the cliff of Nanny Beam's house to watch the sun slowly set across the sea.

"Mum, can I ask you a question?"

She nodded.

"Are you scared?" I asked quietly. "The Light of the World is the source of our powers."

She hesitated. "A little. Everyone gets scared sometimes. We've got a long road ahead, Aurora. But we'll get there."

I didn't say anything and she watched me carefully.

"Everything will be OK, Aurora, you know that, don't you? How could it not be? Just look around you."

I moved my gaze from the sunshine across to Nanny Beam teaching Suzie, Fred and JJ to high kick while Kimmy barked in encouragement, up to Kizzy and Georgie laughing their heads off at something Cherry had said, and then to Dad and Alexis who emerged from the cottage with Clara. She was holding a thick wad of paper in her hands, chatting excitedly.

"You have a point," I agreed with a grin.

"It has been quite the summer," Mum said gently. "Are you sad that it's over?"

I closed my eyes and took a moment to think about my answer, enjoying the warmth of the last rays of sunshine on my face.

"No, not really." I smiled, leaning against her happily. "It's about time for the next adventure."

THE DAILY

Rain Forests.
Norther

Experts attempt to ex

Excl-

Scientists across the world are still trying their
the bizarre sighting earlier this week of th
over the Caribbean.

Sometimes referred to as an aurora
phenomenon is predominantly see
the planet, such as the Arctic, b
recorded a similar light displa

SCOPE

Reefs and...
Lights?!

...n Caribbean phenomenon

Report by Henry Nib

"It makes no sense," Gilbert Granite, a distinguished professor of the sciences stated. "We are as yet unable to understand the mysterious glowing arc that appeared over Jamaica only a few days ago and has now vanished."

...explain
...rn lights

...ous polar light
...latitude regions of
...eek several witnesses
...amaica.

THE WEEKL

FREE AS

OSTRIC
DRIVIN

Questions have been raised after several reported sightings of an ostrich, behind the wheel of a neon-pink sports car, flying in the airs ac above Cornwall and Devon.

This bizarre claim has supported by many witnesse

HERALD

A BIRD!

SPOTTED
FLYING CAR!

al Report by Olive Folio

ocked to social media to comment
on such a sight.

"The ostrich was wearing a
snorkel; I saw him through my
binoculars!" one witness revealed.

"When he saw me staring up at him,
he tooted loudly on the horn."

The *Weekly Herald* has contacted the
prime minister for a statement.

In the meantime, we ask our
readers to be extremely vigilant and
report any ostrich sightings
immediately. The safety of the
country is at stake!

ACKNOWLEDGEMENTS

It has been such a blessing to be able to create children's books, I have loved every single minute of this process and that is down to some pretty awesome people! Thank you to the fabulous team at Scholastic who are so passionate about Lightning Girl, they have worked so hard to make every aspect of this book nothing short of perfection. Thank you for making me feel so welcome and thank you for the very cool Lightning Girl sneakers, ha ha! Lauren Fortune, Aimee Stewart, Rachel Phillipps, Róisín O'Shea, Rachel Partridge, Andrew Biscomb, Eishar Brar: here's to another amazing ride with Aurora Beam and the gang, I'm so excited, love you guys.

Katy Birchall, the superstar! I am in awe of your talent and organizational skills. Thank you once again for breathing life and energy into Lightning Girl, I literally couldn't do it without you!

A huge thank you to the very talented James Lancett. You have brilliantly captured the essence of my characters and brought my vision to life!

A special thank you to
Lauren-with-the-great-ideas-Gardner!
I could not be more thrilled with everything
and you have played a huge part in all of this.

Thank you to all the readers!
For your love, your reviews and your kind
words. It makes me so happy to receive letters
from parents telling me how much their children
enjoyed the first book and whether it's inspired
them to read for the first time or they can identify
with a character, this makes it all worthwhile.
It keeps me highly motivated and determined
to continue to create stories and characters that
inspire children all around the world. I want
them to know their worth, make good choices
and go for their dreams. Children need to
be inspired and if Lightning Girl can play a
part in that, then that makes me so happy.

To all my friends and family, thank you for
your encouragement and support and for
sharing my excitement for this project.

HAPPY READING :)

SUPERHERO STATS

BENJAMIN JACKSON JR. ("JJ")

★ **HEIGHT:** 5 ft. 3 inches

★ **KNOWN FOR:** Super strength

★ **COULDN'T LIVE WITHOUT:** SPORTS!

SUPERHERO STATS

Cherry Mirella

⁕ **HEIGHT:** 5 ft. 1 inch

⁕ **KNOWN FOR:** Supersonic hearing and occasional premonitions

⁕ **COULDN'T LIVE WITHOUT:** Her custom headphones

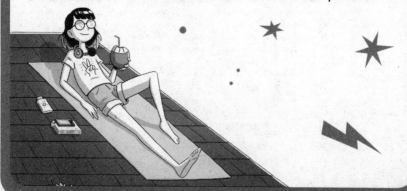

THE BRIGHT SPARKS

Aurora Beam:
Lightning Girl

Fred Pepe: President
of the Bright Sparks

Cherry Mirella

Benjamin Jackson Jr.
("JJ")

Georgie Taylor:
Stylist

Kizzy Carpenter:
The Brains

Kimmy

Suzie Bravo/Flexi-Girl

UNBREAKABLE PINKY PROMISE!

THE BRIGHT SPARKS CODE OF CONDUCT

Never let Aurora go on TV.

1. ~~Keep Aurora's powers TOP SECRET.~~

2. No secrets between members of the Bright Sparks.

3. Never trust a science teacher.

4. Follow Georgie's fashion advice.

See number 1

5. ~~Keep Aurora's powers TOP SECRET!!~~

Photo by John Wright

ALESHA DIXON first found fame as part of Brit-nominated and Mobo Award-winning group Mis-teeq, which achieved 2 platinum albums and 7 top ten hits, before going on to become a platinum-selling solo artist in her own right. Alesha's appearance on *Strictly Come Dancing* in 2007 led to her winning the series and becoming a judge for three seasons.

Since then she has presented and hosted many TV shows including CBBC dance show *Alesha's Street Dance Stars*, *Children In Need*, *Sport Relief*, *Your Face Sounds Familiar* and ITV's *Dance, Dance, Dance*. She is a hugely popular judge on *Britain's Got Talent*.

"My inspiration to create a superhero called Lightning Girl began with wanting my young daughter to feel empowered. It's been a dream to create a strong role model that any child can look up to - I want my readers to see themselves in Aurora, who is dealing with trouble at home and trouble at school alongside her new powers.

I also have a love of precious stones and their healing properties; I have always been fascinated with their spectacular colors and the positive energy that they bring. As human beings we are always searching for something greater within ourselves and a deeper meaning to life and it's my belief that we all have a light within us that can affect change and bring good to the world... we just have to harness it! :)

Enter **AURORA BEAM!**"

Photo by Ian Arnold

Katy Birchall is the author of the side-splittingly funny
The It Girl: Superstar Geek, *The It Girl: Team Awkward,*
The It Girl: Don't Tell the Bridesmaid and *Secrets of*
a Teenage Heiress.

Katy won the 24/7 Theater Festival Award for Most
Promising New Comedy Writer with her very serious
play about a ninja monkey at a dinner party.

Her pet Labradors are the loves of her life, she is
mildly obsessed with Jane Austen and one day she hopes
to wake up as an elf in *The Lord of the Rings.*

LIGHTNING STRIKES TWICE!
READ THEM BOTH.